Acclaim for H. T. Tsiang and
The Hanging on Union Square

"I finished H. T. Tsiang's masterpiece a few hours ago, and I'm still not sure where I am and what day this is. My mind has been picked apart and reassembled. I need a drink."
— Gary Shteyngart, author of *Super Sad True Love Story*

"[Tsiang] was radiant, boisterous, unforgettable."
—*The New Yorker*

"This is a voice to which the white world . . . will have to listen more and more as time passes."
—Upton Sinclair

"Tsiang's writings are quintessentially of the intermingled (and dangerous) public street culture of downtown Manhattan creative life. He carried the mantle, unknowingly, of Wong Chin Foo—who five decades earlier challenged Denis Kearney to a duel with Irish potatoes at Cooper Union's Great Hall. And we, the Mr. Nut faction of the Asian American movement, carry on Tsiang's spirit!"
—John Kuo Wei Tchen, author of *New York Before Chinatown: Orientalism and the Shaping of American Culture, 1776–1882*

"An artist of distinction, H. T. Tsiang created a genre unto itself in 1935 with *The Hanging on Union Square*. Its republication after seventy-five years rescues—from an outlaw existence—a strangely and beautifully evocative satiric allegory."
—Alan Wald, author of *American Night: The Literary Left in the Era of the Cold War*

"[*The Hanging on Union Square*] is original in form without being labored; and it's remarkable for its whimsical insights into various strata of society and for its flashing counterpoint of almost savage sensuality and delicate pity. Throughout, it is alive and evocative. Mr. Tsiang's fanciful and often fantastic visions . . . convey more truth than a shelf of reportorial novels."

—Waldo Frank

"[*The Hanging on Union Square*] felt like slipping into another person's hallucination."

—Hua Hsu, from the Introduction

"[A] masterwork."

—Floyd Cheung, from the Afterword

PENGUIN  CLASSICS

THE HANGING ON UNION SQUARE

H. T. TSIANG (1899–1971) was born in China and emigrated to the United States at the age of twenty-seven. He studied at Stanford and Columbia, and while living in New York he wrote poetry and op-eds, acted in local theater productions, and washed dishes in a Greenwich Village nightclub. Faced with countless rejections from publishers, he self-published three novels, hawking them at downtown political meetings. He also appeared as an actor in Hollywood, most notably in the film *Tokyo Rose,* and in 1943 he staged a theatrical adaptation of *The Hanging on Union Square* in Los Angeles that counted Alfred Hitchcock, Gregory Peck, Orson Welles, and Rita Hayworth among its audience members during its five-year run. He died in Los Angeles.

FLOYD CHEUNG is a professor of English and American studies at Smith College. Coeditor and contributor to *Recovered Legacies: Authority and Identity in Early Asian Literature,* he has worked on the recovery of H. T. Tsiang, Sadakichi Hartmann, Kathleen Tamagawa, John Okada, Munio Makuuchi, and others.

HUA HSU is a staff writer at *The New Yorker,* an associate professor of English at Vassar College, and the author of *A Floating Chinaman: Fantasy and Failure Across the Pacific.*

H. T. TSIANG

The Hanging on Union Square

AN AMERICAN EPIC

Edited with an Afterword and Notes by FLOYD CHEUNG

Introduction by HUA HSU

PENGUIN BOOKS

PENGUIN BOOKS

An imprint of Penguin Random House LLC
penguinrandomhouse.com

First published in the United States of America by H. T. Tsiang 1935
Edition with an introduction by Hua Hsu and an afterword and
notes by Floyd Cheung published by Kaya Press 2013
Published in Penguin Books 2019

Introduction, afterword, and notes published by arrangement with Kaya Press

LIBRARY OF CONGRESS CATALOGING-IN-PUBLICATION DATA
Names: Tsiang, H. T., 1899–1971, author. | Cheung, Floyd, 1969– editor,
writer of afterword, writer of added commentary. | Hsu, Hua, 1977– writer of introduction.
Title: The hanging on Union Square : an American epic / H.T. Tsiang ;
edited with an afterword and notes by Floyd Cheung ; introduction by Hua Hsu.
Description: [New York, New York] : Penguin Books, 2019. |
Includes bibliographical references.
Identifiers: LCCN 2019007510 (print) | LCCN 2019011040 (ebook) |
ISBN 9780525505808 (ebook) | ISBN 9780143134022 (paperback) |
Subjects: LCSH: Union Square (New York, N.Y.)—Fiction.
Classification: LCC PS3539.S53 (ebook) | LCC PS3539.S53 H36 2019 (print) |
DDC 813/.52—dc23
LC record available at https://lccn.loc.gov/2019007510

Set in Sabon LT Std

146119709

Contents

THE HANGING ON UNION SQUARE

Act I

Act II

Act III

Act IV

Introduction

Thanks but No Thanks but Thanks

Writers deal with rejection in different ways. Some shred or delete their rejection letters instantly, lest material evidence of onetime failure remain; others bury them deep in drawers or file them away in obscure corners of their hard drive, revisiting them only in the light of later glory. It might be an occasion for fellowship on one of those websites devoted to sharing and laughing at the way work has been declined through the ages. The wild few fire back angry ripostes or desperate clarifications. You would be surprised by all the folders full of such postcards and notes that remain in the university archives of writers whom history records as world-conquerors.

The point is that few people enjoy being told that what they've written is too strange or unsuitable for publication or, worse yet, beyond salvage, thanks for the inquiry and kindly lose this address. And nobody excerpts these rejection letters on the back covers and inner pages of their books, where blurbs customarily go.

I became fascinated with the Chinese American writer H. T. Tsiang when I found a first edition of *The Hanging on Union Square*, which he self-published in 1935. It felt like slipping into another person's hallucination. The front cover was mysteriously confrontational and free of any useful information such as a title or author's name. Instead, three blocks of text which resembled a madman's conversation with himself—"YES the cover of a book is more of a book than the book is a book," "I say—NO," "SO." This last word then stretched itself out and colonized the entire back cover. Opening the book and browsing its first few pages, I was ambushed by more signs of Tsiang's unusual, stubborn mind: a page of tepid, bemused half-praise from the likes of Granville Hicks, Carl van Doren, and Louis Adamic, followed by another page excerpting rejection notices he had received from various publishers. I sought out other Tsiang novels. There was *China Red*, self-published in 1931, with its crude, hand-drawn art and back-cover blurbs doubting its "popular appeal." He finally found a proper publisher for 1937's *And China Has Hands*, but the dust jacket reprints a letter from Tsiang in which he offers some input on the dust jacket's layout. These works didn't fit into any available categories of immigrant writing or proletarian art. But then his biography didn't follow the paths taken by most twentieth-century Chinese Americans either.

Tsiang was born "in a small hut" near Shanghai in 1899 and died decades later in Hollywood, a local oddball and occasional movie actor known around town for the R-rated, one-man, one-hour adaptation of Hamlet he performed every Friday night for a dozen years. He worked for a brief spell as Sun Yat-sen's secretary before fractures within the Kuomintang—as well as his own outspokenness about the party's shifting ideologies—forced him to emigrate to the United States in 1926. He spent time in California's Bay Area and then New York City, living the itinerant life of a graduate student. Encouraged by some of his professors at Columbia and the New School to channel his left-leaning politics into creative forms, he began writing and publishing poetry in the late 1920s. He eventually moved to fiction.

Collectively, Tsiang's works do not seem to comprise a coherent oeuvre. They suggest a promiscuous attitude toward standards of form and genre. No existing literary approaches suited Tsiang's spectacularly expansive vision of how the world should be, and this might explain why he ranged so freely from sentimental, epistolary novels to militantly leftist poetry, plays, and music, to bitterly ironic, experimental novels. He enjoyed very little success, even within the hospitable climate of New York's interwar proletarian arts scene.

Not that Tsiang felt chastened. Anyone who picks up a pen possesses a healthier than average ego, and despite a steady stream of baffled rejection letters, he continued to believe that he had something important to share. These frustrations only refined his critical instincts. His works came to express a frustration with New York's proletarian dogma, which, despite an inherent hope for global solidarity, privileged the American urban experience. Tsiang's other natural audience—those interested in China—ignored him as well, opting instead for the more palatable visions of Pearl Buck (whom he would frequently mock in his novels) and the professionalized establishment of China-watchers.

If anything, these frustrations animated Tsiang and pushed him toward increasingly experimental ends. His characters descended into ever more desperate, absurd situations that seemed to reflect his own sense of alienation. In particular, he became obsessed with what a book was, not simply as pages housing content—ideas, characters, plot, etc.—but as an object entering into a marketplace as well. By the time Tsiang published *The Hanging on Union Square* in 1935, he seemed resigned to the reality that no publisher, regardless of political orientation, would accept his work, which could go from whimsical and trippy to vengeful and brutish in a matter of paragraphs. It seemed that publishers and editors couldn't tell whether his style was banal or experimental—the word that keeps showing up in their letters is "interesting."

From the first page, *Hanging* is desperate to flaunt its convictions. That's not quite right. It's more of a performance of desperation, a need to be recognized for having convictions, no matter how basic (in this case, money = evil) they may be. It's a challenge to the reader: do you care as much as I do?

Hanging chronicles a day in the life of the lonely, unemployed Mr. Nut. We find him in a workers' cafeteria, listening to the sad fates of those around him, wondering to himself how he will get by without a steady job. Unlike everyone else, however, Nut has yet to surrender his by-the-bootstraps idealism. He insists that his poverty is only temporary and that he will one day leave this all behind. Aspiration becomes an affliction. His mind swirls with dreams of striking it rich, the mantra overtaking all reason or logic, like *Ragged Dick* rewritten by Gertrude Stein.

Perhaps this is what has driven him mad. Over a chilling, misadventure-filled night adrift in the city, he encounters the winners and the losers, the weird and the depraved: screwball book critics, dirty old men, a self-obsessed poet yearning for a connection ("I wish your taste would be like mine—/We could just be sixty-nine"), disgraced millionaires, comically selfless communists, the shadow government playing the rest of us like puppets. Nut even encounters Tsiang himself. The depiction is far from flattering: Tsiang floats through his own novel as an irritating and obnoxious crank trying to convince someone to buy a weathered copy of his previous self-published opus, *China Red*.

Suffice it to say that Nut eventually sheds the cynicism he initially feels toward the cause of the "masses." Yet joining the party rank-and-file doesn't suit him. His growing sense of abjection seems to have a euphoric, liberating effect on him. Freed from his desire to change his own situation, he aspires instead to change the world. The last few chapters of *Hanging*, as Nut comes to accept his fate, are hysterical and absurd, yet strangely moving.

Anyone who self-publishes an "American Epic" is worth investigating, especially when they seem to luxuriate in their own marginality. It's hard to imagine a more appropriate time for a *Hanging* reprint, as the populist rage of the last few years challenges us to imagine new ways of communicating with the masses. Tsiang's desire to appoint himself Everyman—to yell and argue and rage on behalf of all downtrodden brothers and sisters—might as well be happening today; the same applies to his ultimate failure. Perhaps Nut's increasing darkness doesn't suggest a way forward. But the quality of his desperation—a proxy for Tsiang's, perhaps—still hold. We live in a time when self-publishing is no longer a last resort, and a contemporary reader will probably be more hospitable to *Hanging*'s stubborn weirdness than the readers and publishers of Tsiang's time. This isn't to say that we've caught up to Tsiang—this would imply that he possessed some coherent vision of the world—just that his manic collision of ideas and feelings seems deeply familiar, as does his dense mix of irony and earnestness, his experimental playfulness and all-at-once frustration that nobody is listening.

Following the pages of rejections that open *Hanging*'s first edition, Tsiang offered a brief note addressed directly to the reader. "The writer takes this opportunity of conveying his deep appreciation of the kindness of the various critics and publishers who had read his manuscript," he writes with a seeming sincerity. But maybe they can just agree to disagree—this is the book he wants to write, even if nobody wants to publish it. "Stubbornly or nuttily," he explains, he is compelled to advance his vision in its purest, uncut form, outside of the publishing industry that enforces our sense of the mainstream. Failure may be inevitable; perhaps he even courts it. But he is unafraid. After all, "the reaction of the masses can't be wrong."

HUA HSU

Acknowledgments

For providing access to archival material, I would like to thank the following individuals and institutions: Doug Capra, Pierre Ferrand, Fred Ho, the Mortimer Rare Book Room of Smith College, the New York Public Library, and the Smithsonian Institution. For providing research assistance, I would like to thank Ariel Endlich-Frazier, Stefanie Grindle, Judy Lei, Elizabeth Mincer, Mara Pagano, Lisa Yvonne Ramos, Pamela Skinner, Sara Studebaker, Amy Teutemacher, and Katarina Yuan. Thanks go also to Sunyoung Lee of Kaya Press for guiding this volume through the publication process; Hua Hsu for writing this volume's introduction; the Smith College Committee on Faculty Compensation and Development and the Woodrow Wilson National Fellowship Foundation for funding portions of my research; my colleagues at Smith College and the Five-College Asian/Pacific/American Studies Program for encouraging my work; and Sheri Cheung for being my first and best reader.

FLOYD CHEUNG

Chronology

1899   The son of a grain store worker and a maid,
H. T. Tsiang (Jiang Xizeng) is born on May 3 in
Qi'an, a village in the district of Nantong,
Jiangsu Province in China.

1908   Tsiang's father dies.

1911   Chinese Revolution led by Sun Yat-sen ends rule of
Qing Dynasty; Kuomintang (Nationalist Party)
established.

1912   Tsiang's mother dies.

1913   According to his sister, Tsiang could read English by
this time. He attends the Tongzhou Teachers' School
in Jiangsu on scholarship.

1915   Besides studying, Tsiang protests against the practice
of female foot-binding and the Twenty-One Demands
issued by the Japanese government to the Chinese
government on January 18. Many Chinese detested
these demands that lands, resources, and rights be
given over to Japan. Tsiang is arrested but freed
thanks to his schoolmaster.

1917   Bolshevik Revolution led by Vladimir Lenin inspires
Tsiang. He is particularly taken with Lenin's idea of

"world revolution," expressed in *Imperialism, the Highest Stage of Capitalism.*

1918   Sun Yat-sen sends congratulations to Lenin.

1925   Tsiang earns a bachelor's degree in political economy at Southeastern University in Nanjing.
     He works briefly as secretary to Sun Yat-sen before the latter dies of cancer in March. Chiang Kai-shek takes over control of the Kuomintang and swings the party away from communism. Tsiang critiques this move and receives threats to his life. He faces "the executioner's axe at home."

1926   Fails to migrate to the Soviet Union and so enters the United States as a student, enrolling at Stanford University.
     Tsiang works for a short time as associate editor for the Kuomintang organ *Young China* and then helps to found a bilingual periodical, *Chinese Guide in America*, which is critical of the Kuomintang and goes so far as to call Chiang Kai-shek a "traitor."

1927   The May 1 issue of the *Chinese Guide in America* reports that a mob attacked Tsiang and others while they were distributing leaflets critical of the Chinese government.

1928   On February 26, Tsiang is arrested for planning a demonstration against Chow Loo, a Kuomintang official. The *Los Angeles Times* calls Tsiang, "the leader of the radicals."
     Tsiang moves to New York and enrolls at Columbia, where he takes courses in public law, economics, history, and literature.

1928   Self-publishes *Poems of the Chinese Revolution* after having published five individual poems in the *Daily*

Worker and the *New Masses*. Upton Sinclair writes, "What he has written is not perfect poetry, but it is the perfect voice of Young China, protesting against the lot of the underdog."

1931   Self-publishes *China Red*. Tsiang works as a dishwasher at the Howdy Club in Greenwich Village, where he is permitted to give a reading from his novel.

1933   Radiana Pazmor sings arrangements of Tsiang's poems "Chinaman, Laundryman" as well as "Sacco, Vanzetti" by Ruth Crawford Seeger at the Mellon Gallery in Philadelphia and Carnegie Hall in New York.
       On May 21, Tsiang, along with 30 other poets, posts his poems in Washington Square in New York and discusses them with passers-by.

1934   Pete Seeger sets Tsiang's poem "Lenin! Who's That Guy" to music and includes it in the *Workers Song Book*.

1935   Self-publishes *The Hanging on Union Square*.

1937   Robert Speller publishes *And China Has Hands*.
       On July 7, the Second Sino-Japanese War officially begins. The two countries had been fighting intermittently since 1931.
       Tsiang lectures on the question "Should the U.S. interfere in the Chinese-Japanese Conflict?" at the Thomas Paine Society on December 10.

1938   Self-publishes *China Marches On*. The play adapts the legend of Fa Mulan to tell the story of the dare-to-die military squad that valiantly defended its position in Shanghai against an overwhelming Japanese force in 1937.

On January 4, Tsiang speaks on "The Arts in China Today" for the Federal Theatre Project of the Works Progress Administration on radio station WQXR.

1939   Produces *China Marches On* and *The Hanging on Union Square* as plays at the Irving Plaza in New York.

Beginning in October, Tsiang is imprisoned at the Ellis Island detention center, ostensibly for failing to re-enroll at Columbia University and hence maintain his exemption status as a student. The American Committee for Protection of Foreign Born retains attorney Ira Gollobin to aid him.

1940   Released from detention and granted a six-month reprieve.

1941   Imprisoned again at the Ellis Island detention center while awaiting deportation. Tsiang begins correspondence with Rockwell Kent, appealing for his help. While in detention, Tsiang also composes poetry, some on toilet paper. He also writes President Franklin Roosevelt on May 30 to criticize U.S. arms sales to Japan. Through Kent's connections and the efforts of the American Committee for Protection of Foreign Born, Tsiang is released. In August, he visits Kent in Ausable Forks, New York. On scholarship, he enrolls at the New School for Social Research to work with Erwin Piscator, innovator of the agitprop play.

1942   Acts in a 5-minute version of *China Marches On* and a 41-minute version of *The Hanging on Union Square* in Piscator's Dramatic Workshop.

1943   Acts in the film *Behind the Rising Sun*.

1944   Plays Mr. Nut in *The Hanging on Union Square* in
       Los Angeles.
            Also acts in films *The Purple Heart, The Keys of
       the Kingdom,* and *Thirty Seconds over Tokyo.*

1945   Produces *China Marches On* and *The Hanging on
       Union Square* with the Chinese American
       Theater at the California Labor School in San
       Francisco, working with actors Benson Fong,
       Keye Luke, Richard Loo, and James Wong
       Howe.
            Also acts in films *China Sky* and *China's Little
       Devils.*

1946   Acts in films *Tokyo Rose* and *In Old Sacramento.*

1947   Acts in films *Black Gold, Singapore, Little Mister
       Jim,* and *The Beginning or the End.*

1948   Produces *The Hanging on Union Square* and *Canton
       Rickshaw* at the Rainbow-Etienne Studio in
       Hollywood.
            Also acts in the film *The Babe Ruth Story.*

1949   Acts in films *State Department: File 649* and *Chicken
       Every Sunday.*

1950-60s   Continues to act in films like *Panic in the Streets*
       and *Oceans Eleven,* as well as television series like
       Gunsmoke, I Spy, My Three Sons, and *Bonanza.*
            Variety reports that for twelve years, Tsiang
       performs a "one-hour, one-man performance of
       Hamlet at the Rainbow Theatre [in Hollywood] every
       Friday night."

1971   Dies in Los Angeles on July 16.

The Hanging on
Union Square

What is unsaid
Says,
And says more
Than what is said.

SAYS I

ACT I

1:

HE WAS GROUCHING

. . . A ten-cent check,
  I had my coffee an'
  I have only a nickel
  In my hand.

Money makes money; no money makes no money.
  Money talks; no money, no talking; talking produces no money.

He is worrying; he has no money.
  He is crying; he lost money.
  He is smiling; he made money.

Isn't she a beautiful girl? I wish I had money.
  He is a nice-looking fellow. Has he any money?
  He marries an old maid; the old maid has money.
  She marries an old bald-head, fat-belly; the old bald-head, fat-belly has money.
  He likes this girl. He likes the other girl. He likes the other girl better than this girl. The other girl has more money than this girl.
  She likes this fellow. She likes the other fellow. She likes the other fellow better than this fellow. The other fellow has more money than this fellow.

It is the same girl. Today she has money. She is a Honey Darling. Tomorrow she has no money. She is a Daughter of a Bitch.
  It is the same fellow. Today he has money. He is a Honey Darling. Tomorrow he has no money. He is a Son Of . . .

An old fellow kneeling in front of a young fellow. Fooling with his shoes. The old fellow wants to make a nickel of money. Rubbing. Brushing. Carefully! Respectfully! The old fellow expects a nickel tip-money.

The girls in the next door burlesque show with nothing on except their natural skins. Shaking breasts. Moving hips. Sparkling eyes. Front going up and down. Before a lip-parted and mouth-watering audience. Making money.

That fellow doesn't talk to me any more. I didn't let him have a nickel of money.

This fellow is so friendly to me. I once treated him to coffee. One nickel of money.

He smokes no more cigarettes. Cigarettes cost too much money. He smokes a pipe now. Pipes cost less money.

Smoke cigarettes, somebody spends your money. Smoke a pipe, you alone spend your money.

The guy writes no more poetry. In poetry, there is no money.

The fellow writes sex stories. Sex is depression proof.

He hangs around Union Square. He has no money.

He disappears from Union Square. He has made a little money.

Bedbugs bite me. I have no money. Bedbugs don't bite Rockefeller.[1] Rockefeller has money.

Rich men go to Heaven. Rich men have money. Poor men don't go to Heaven. Poor men have no money.

Three-dollar shoes; three-dollar feet. Ten-dollar shoes; ten-dollar feet. There are million-dollar feet. There are no million-dollar shoes. The shoemakers must be crazy. They don't know how to make money!

He has money: he lives on Park Avenue. He lives on Park Avenue: he sees no one who has no money. He sees no one who

has no money: he thinks everywhere is Park Avenue and everyone, everywhere, has as much money as everyone who lives on
Park Avenue.

He is radical; he has no money.
    He is conservative; he has money.
    He is wishy-washy; he has a wishy-washy amount of money.

He has more money; he is more conservative.
    He has more more money; he is more more conservative.
    He has more more and more money; he is more more and
    more conservative.

He has no money. Yet he is conservative. He expects someday
to have money. He expects someday to have lots of money.
    He has money. He has lots of money. Yet he is radical. Rad-
ical talk costs him no money.
    I don't like money. You don't like money. He doesn't like
money.
    You have money. He has money. I must have money.

It's under this system!
    It's under this system!

Mr. System
    Beware:
    The Hanging
    On
    Union Square! . . .

II:

ONCE IN A COMMUNIST CAFETERIA

"A ten-cent check,
I had my coffee an'
I have only a nickel
In my hand."

It was Mr. Nut grouching.

Mr. Nut was grouching about his being stuck in a cafeteria on Fourteenth Street.

This situation made Mr. Nut think more or less differently from when, three months ago, he visited a Communist Cafeteria on Thirteenth Street.

Everybody there called him "Comrade." "Comrade" this. "Comrade" that. To people in the Communist Cafeteria, Mr. Nut wasn't "Mister" anymore. It did not please him; for how could they take for granted so much that he was their "comrade"—a Communist?

Sometimes they called Mr. Nut "Fellow-Worker." That made him madder still. How could they know that he was a worker? Did they not see that he had a black derby on! Yes, he was a worker. Now. For the time being! But how could they tell that he would not, someday, by saving some money, establish a business of his own?

In the Communist Cafeteria, there were so many literature agents, so many pamphlet-salesmen and so many contribution-seekers. One after the other.

If a panhandler came to you, all you needed was to show

him your face—he would go away. No argument. But these agents, salesmen and contribution-seekers gave you more trouble than panhandlers. Why? Because, they said, they themselves would get nothing out of it. Every cent would go to the cause. Was it true? Yes. It was true. For all these sealed tin-boxes with coin-spaces at the tops and the contribution-lists were their spokesmen. Besides, they wouldn't ask you to buy or to contribute right away. They just sat at your table and made friends with you. And explained things to you. A few seconds or a minute later, the boxes, the pamphlet and the contribution-list appeared from some unseen source.

With your hand, you said, "I won't give." But your conscience said, "I must do my share." And you lost money.

On the wall there was a sign: "Don't shout so loud, your comrade can hear you!" Mr. Nut thought: "If the Communists don't shout, how can they make a revolution?"

Again, he saw on the wall many figures, painted on cardboard; figures with overalls on. Shirt-sleeves rolled up. Chests bare. Black hair could be seen. Caps incorrectly placed. Shoes out of shape. Yes, these figures looked like him when he was working. But he did not understand why the fellow who made those posters could not do the worker a favor by giving him a necktie, a coat, pressed trousers, a nice, soft, felt hat or a derby. It needn't have cost him more than a few strokes.

About six o'clock, the floor-manager, moving from one table to another, was propagandizing: "This is no private business. This is your restaurant." (Does that mean that Nut will not have to pay for all he ate?) "After you eat, don't hang around. Give your seats to others. We're not capitalists. We can't afford to lose money. Comrades!" (Again Comrade.) "Fellow-workers!" (Again Fellow-worker).

If the so-called "comrade'" floor-manager had had a butcher face, Mr. Nut would have had a chance to show his anger. But the so-called "comrade" was smiling. What could Mr. Nut do? The point was, however, that while Mr. Nut came here to get some Communistic atmosphere, although two hours had elapsed, he hadn't seen the whole thing yet. But Mr. Nut had to move.

As to one thing he felt he had been educated.

While he was conversing with a young fellow in the cafeteria, Nut interrogated him with: "How's business?" Upon hearing this, the color of the young fellow's face suddenly changed and his eyebrows rose. The dark spots of his eyes became steady and because of the steadiness it made the surrounding white parts appear smaller. Mr. Nut knew that the young fellow was angry. But Mr. Nut didn't know why.

The young fellow saw that that Mr. Nut was shooting back with a steady face, too, and he became more angry. Because of his doubled anger, the young fellow pointed to Mr. Nut saying: "You are a Mister! You are a Boss! You are a Capitalist!" and "You are a Business Man!"

Now Mr. Nut stood up and shouted with joy. For it was the first time in his life that there was a person who didn't call him "Nut" and gave him instead such respectable titles as "Boss," "Business Man" and even "Capitalist."

He held the pointing fingers of the outstretched hand of the young fellow warmly and tightly and said to him: "You know me better than my father and mother when they were alive, and you are my friend—my best friend. You know that I am not a Nut. I will have my day. In return, I, too, wish you success and that you will make lots of money."

The young fellow having heard all that Mr. Nut said to him, every word, didn't like it. But the young fellow understood that Mr. Nut was not sarcastic or sneering, nor had any bad feeling; for the young fellow saw his face blank, his eyes sincere, his forehead perspiring. And he felt his hand warm and heard his breath short.

Then the young fellow replied with the same sincerity and said: "Please call me 'Thief,' 'Robber,' and all kinds of other names, but not 'Business Man' or 'Capitalist.' I am a League member;[2] I am a young Communist!"

Mr. Nut didn't know what that was all about. But Mr. Nut did know that Communists do not like the daily compliment: "How is business!"

Then he heard a girl call out to that young fellow, "We have to be at the meeting earlier. So the boys can not say we girls are inferior. Comrade Stubborn: Hurry up." Nut now understood that that young fellow was not a fellow but a girl. A girl in a certain kind of uniform. He suddenly felt that this talking, finger-holding, eye-to-eye-looking and all this sorrow, joy, sentiment and emotion should not have been expressed.

III:

WITH A TEMPERAMENT
OF THIS SORT

"A ten-cent check
I had my coffee an'
I have only a nickel
In my hand."

The reason Nut was called Nut was very interesting.

Once Mr. Nut shaved all the hair off his head. Some say he did it for the sake of a sun-bath. Since other parts of the body needed a sun-bath there was no reason why this part of the body shouldn't need one.

Some say Mr. Nut shaved all the hair off his head because he knew that he had no money now. But he did believe that some day he would have money like other bald-headed millionaires walking with pretty movie-stars along Park Avenue. But he would not have his head bald then. It would be too awkward. In order to avoid awkwardness in the future, he did the prevention-work early. The more you shaved your hair, the stronger it would become. It was the same with the hair as with the beard.

Some say he shaved all the hair off his head because his friend Mr. Wiseguy once cut off some while he was napping. He had all his hair shaved off as a form of protest—passive resistance.

Some say he shaved all the hair off his head because so many girls liked him. So many girls liked him so much, his hair was souvenired off.

No matter what the reason may have been, when his hair was shaved off and his head became nut-like, he won the title "Nut."

Many millionaires are Nut-headed. Yet they are not Nut-named. As far as Mr. Nut was concerned, there were other stories involved.

Once he was standing at the corner of Fourteenth Street and Union Square. A bus was passing by. A girl in the rear seat waved her hand at him. She smiled too. When he began to wave his hand and smile, the bus began to move. He moved too. But the bus had four wheels. He had only two.

Every day after work, he came to the same spot, waiting. Yes, there were some girls in the bus. Yes, they were smiling. Yes, a few of them were waving their hands, too. But they had nothing to do with him. Yes, sometimes some of them were waving their hands and smiling at *him* too. But none of them was the girl he had seen. He wanted to ask the conductor, but he didn't know how. At last he described the situation to the conductor. The conductor told him to go to the Nut House.

In the cafeteria, nobody stopped you from looking at the girls. Some fellows had the ability of moving only their eyeballs. They could see what they wanted to see without being noticed. But the muscles of Mr. Nut's eyes were not well developed. He had to move his head. He had to move the trunk of his body. Others moved their heads and trunks too. But they had the ability to generalize. They had the whole picture in a glance and digested it later. So these fellows did not take much time. But Mr. Nut was too scientific. And after these scientific studies, or, you may say, these artistic appreciations, Mr. Nut had a critical opinion. And in addition to the critical opinion, he had his constructive suggestion. It is said that once he suggested to a young girl that the seams of her stockings were not properly placed along the back of her legs. The reward was: "Mind your own business, Nut!"

Once in a cafeteria, Mr. Wiseguy spoke about his Four F theory regarding the technique of handling a woman. Others, hearing his theory, laughed and laughed to show their approval and appreciation. But to Mr. Nut it was as hard as the theory of relativity.

He asked what the theory of the Four F's was about.

Mr. Wiseguy told him that the first F was "To Find."

Mr. Nut would have liked to know where; but Mr. Wiseguy proceeded with his second F: "To Fool." Mr. Nut was surprised that one person had to fool the other. The others exclaimed unanimously, "That is the way it ought to be."

Mr. Nut asked about the third F. Mr. Wiseguy turned his head around and suddenly stopped—because a few girls sat behind. Mr. Nut asked again. Mr. Wiseguy said the fourth F was "To Forget."

Nut said: "How can I forget, when you haven't told me the third F yet?" Mr. Wiseguy raised a fork and said in anger: "You understand? Nut!"

Once he moved from uptown along Forty-second Street to the downtown section. He didn't take a taxi, for it would have cost him one dollar. He took the subway. Bundle after bundle—it took him about fifteen trips to get the work done. Five cents to go down and five cents to come up. So one round-trip cost him ten cents and fifteen trips cost him a dollar-fifty. Still he was pleased. His theory was that a taxi was for a rich man and the subway was for a poor man.

Next day his friend gave him a bed. He knew that this time he could not stick to his previous theory. He called a taxi from uptown Bronx to downtown. That cost him three dollars. And he saw a sign on the window of a neighborhood second-hand furniture store showing the price of the same bed was only one dollar and fifty cents.

The first few nights Mr. Nut was pleased, however, that he slept on a "something-for-nothing" bed. But gradually he became Nut-conscious. How could you say that a dollar and a half extra wasn't Nut money? And no wonder others called him Nut. He would also call himself a Nut. The more he thought of it, the more Nut-conscious he became. The more Nut-conscious he became, the harder it was for him to sleep.

He turned around, from one side to the other. He could not sleep.

Next day he got up early. He looked at the bed. It was the same bed that he could get for a dollar and fifty cents at his neighborhood store. The more he looked at the bed the madder he became. And then, the question was not a matter of a dollar and fifty cents. It was, again, a question of principle. The question of his reputation. The bed wasn't a bed anymore. It was a symbol.

It was symbolizing not one thing only. It was symbolizing many things. It was symbolizing all the humiliation given to him and wrong done to him by others, in his whole life.

Finally he stamped on the bed with his feet. He stamped and stamped till it was out of shape. Then he tied it together and hoisted it to his shoulder. He opened his door, marched toward the East River and dumped it into the water.

Then he felt relieved. For he thought now all his Nutness was gone together with that bed. He was a new man.

With a temperament of this sort, it can be imagined how restless Mr. Nut was now.

I V :

"NO RUSSIAN! NO JEW!"

"A ten-cent check,
I had my coffee an'
I have only a nickel
In my hand."

Mr. Nut was now remembering how that uniformed girl, Stubborn, had become a communist.

Stubborn had the best record in a class of eighty. After her graduation from high-school, she wanted to go to college, so she would be able to prepare herself as a school teacher. That would be a steady job with comparatively good pay, and one could have more chance to play with little children, since she had no brother or sister of her own. But how could she get the money to pay for the expenses of four years even at one of the free city colleges?

Stubborn could not go to college.

She wanted to go to a business school for only one year, in order to get work in an office.

But one year was one year. And because of the depression her father had his pay cut. From fourteen dollars to twelve—and he had to support a family of three!

So Stubborn had to go to work. And right away!

With no special preparation at all, what kind of work could she get?

She got a job in the ticket office of a movie-house, on Fourteenth Street.

For the employment agent thought that for that kind of job one didn't need any brains or education. Just a good face to be looked at. That was enough!

She made ten dollars a week. She was happy. For she was getting almost as much as her father.

When Stubborn first walked to the office the day-shift girl, Miss Digger, looked at her carefully.

Stubborn had an amiable face. Shy eyes. Innocent smile. The dimples in her cheeks appeared and disappeared together with the appearance and disappearance of her smiles.

Her white, small and even teeth were regularly placed between unlipsticked red lips.

With her head a little bent forward, Stubborn gave the appearance of a well-read girl who had an indication of deep thinking. And when her chest stretched and her head went up, again she gave Miss Digger an idea that Stubborn was conscious of her customary unhealthful posture and was doing her correction-work.

Miss Digger looked at Stubborn downwardly. She saw what a nice pair of legs ran down gradually from the edge of a wind-ruffled skirt—narrowly, narrowly and more narrowly and then delicately and solidly linked with a pair of well-proportioned feet, which were comfortably housed in a pair of comfortable walking shoes.

The hair of Stubborn was brunette and was artistically harmonious with a white skin that thinly veiled the rosy color shining underneath.

Miss Digger looked at Stubborn again and again.

Her medium size made Stubborn look even more feminine.

Miss Digger had towards her a certain kind of feeling that she didn't usually have towards her own sex. Respect. Admiration. Pity. Sympathy.

Had not the boss, Mr. System, been standing near, Miss Digger, in addition to giving Stubborn a warm and hearty handshaking, would have embraced and kissed her.

Stubborn worked for a few days. Everything was nice. Except that her boss, Mr. System, told her that she should use lipstick to make her lips redder and use powder to make her face whiter. And that her eyebrows should be painted and should be standing up. And that they should either be widened with an eyebrow pencil or be sliced off and made thin as a line.

In a movie-house the good looks of the cashier are important. And to be so decorated as to catch the attention of the passersby and make them stop and buy tickets, is still more important. The duty of a girl in a movie ticket-box is to be a cashier, model and barker combined.

These things should have been told her by the employment agent or by Miss Digger; but the employment agent thought that she was old enough to know about it herself; and Miss Digger was not generous enough to tell her secrets.

So her boss, Mr. System, told her.

Stubborn did not want to do what he told her. But when she thought of ten dollars a week and how much her family needed it, she did it. But whenever she got out of that box she would wash all her decoration off and then go home.

A few days later, her boss, Mr. System, asked her whether she had a boy friend. And at another time, her boss, Mr. System, asked her how she liked his new car. And at still another time, the boss, Mr. System, asked her how she would like to go out with him and have a nice time. And Mr. System accompanied all these words with a little touch here and there. He even tried to kiss her.

For Heaven's sake! Mr. System, the boss, was old enough to be her father or even her grandfather. His mouth smelt like an ashtray. He had eyes that gleamed and shifted like those of a fox, and irregular teeth as black and dirty as the scraps in a garbage can. After two weeks' patience and suffering, Stubborn exploded suddenly with her soft and determined hand.

She struck his face.

Mr. System could not believe that a shy, quiet, amiable, naive and rather small-sized girl could suddenly be changed into a creature with standing hair, eyes electrified, and so stubborn! And that so delicate and so soft a hand could make his fat, rubber-skinned face feel so hot with pain.

Yet he was capitalistic enough to be patient and without

anger. He said to her: "Say, Miss! I was just kidding you. Don't be so stubborn! Why! But your slaps are nevertheless deliciously appreciated!"

Stubborn lost her job.

Because of her appearance, Stubborn got a job in a movie-house easily. Because of her stubbornness (or revolutionary temperament) she could not keep her job.

Stubborn decided to change her line and become a dressmaker.

She became a Communist when there was a strike in the dressmaking trade. The strike was won and she made fifteen cents more on a dress than before. One dollar more a day and six dollars more a week. That six dollars! Thank God! It was lots of money! She could spend those dollars in a hundred ways. So she belonged to the trade-union.[3] Because she was young she also belonged to the Young Communist League.

"I, Nut, become a radical?" Nut said to himself. "Become a Red? No. No, Siree! I am no Russian! I am no Jew!"

V:

THINKING OF
MR. WISEGUY

"A ten-cent check,
I had my coffee an'
I have only a nickel
In my hand."

How could Mr. Nut get out of this cafeteria? He was thinking of his friend, Mr. Wiseguy.

Mr. Wiseguy was of Anglo-Saxon or Teutonic origin.

But something had gone wrong and his nose was a little bit non-Anglo-Saxon. Or you may say a bit Christ-like. As a result of twenty years' care, finally the lower part of the nose pointed upward instead of downward.

He had trouble with his eyes, too. They were rather small and some people suspected him of being partly Chinese. Every day he had his eye exercise and because of his hard work, the eyeballs, though not deeply-located, were as large as those of the average Anglo-Saxon. Their color was as blue as the water in the sea. Because, whenever he had his face washed, he had his eyes washed at the same time.

He was five feet seven. For the average Anglo-Saxon he was one inch short. This defect had been overcome by shoe-fixing. Additional rubber heels were attached both inside and outside. That made him one inch taller.

His hair was artificially bleached. That made him neither Spanish- nor Italian-looking.

He had a weak chin. So he grew a beard; on the one hand to hide his weakness, and on the other hand to increase his dignity. His mustache had an indefinable style. Sometimes it was Hitler-like. Sometimes it was upturned in the manner of a French count.

The using of his eye-glasses was scientifically studied. Sometimes he had his glasses placed low at the bridge of this nose. When his eyes were lifted up above the glasses, he had the air of a learned professor. Sometimes he put on a monocle over a not deep-set eye and with his body leaning back and head stretched to one side, he gave you a grand impersonation of ex-Police Commissioner Grover Whalen.[4]

His accent was superb. It was a slow, bass, guttural of the Oxford or Harvard style that left the lips unused.

He could speak to all kind of languages. But not so much. Just everyday, necessary phrases equivalent to the English: "How are you?," "Thank you!," "You are the most generous gentleman that I have ever met!," "You are the most beautiful girl that I have ever seen!," "May I have your telephone number and call you when your husband is not in?" and "May I have some small change to have my mustache waxed?"

All his past glories and present prosperity and future hope were keynoted by his way of taking various kinds of cigarettes out of various cigarette cases. Turkish! Spanish! German! Russian! And so on and so forth. When one was not too stupid, one would naturally be tempted to believe that these cigarettes and cigarette-cases were telling you that their present owner had traveled extensively, although they may have come from some five-and-ten-cent store or from the open market at the end of the Williamsburg Bridge.

One also noticed his expensive leather billfold. To pay the amount needed for a newspaper—only two or five cents—he would show his billfold. There were two exceptional occasions when Mr. Wiseguy's billfold got a vacation. One was when no girl friend was in his company. The other was when his creditors approached.

He was a financier of a superior type. He borrowed money from one person and then he borrowed more from another person. Part of the money was used for his daily expenses and the remaining part to pay debts in order to make his credit good. By repeating this procedure Mr. Wiseguy made his living. And at the same time made his credit even better than that of the houses down in Wall Street.

He had lots of newspaper clippings. These clippings were clipped by a most famous institution called The Bureau of Exploitation, which, in commercial language, is the same as Publicity Agent. Because the latter name had been so vulgarized, it had lost its artistic or cultural sense. This organization— The Bureau of Exploitation—made you famous, and successful and got you somewhere.

In the newspaper clippings, such terms as "Sweetest charm," "Marvelous personality," "Exclusive intelligence," "Psychological reincarnation," "Technological and Crazyological Consultations" were mystically printed.

Mr. Wiseguy had a literary appearance. But he was too practical to be sentimental.

Poetry seemed to him to be no more than the yearning of a sex-starved idiot. His address book, from A to Z, was filled with names and he was not in the least hungry.

As to novels, he would say that they were the riskless adventures of an uncourageous maiden, or the companions of a lonely and wealthy wife whose husband was away at a Directors' Meeting.

All Mr. Wiseguy needed was a five-cent telephone call, or a peep across a half-curtained window into another man's lighted apartment where a censor-unreached chapter was coming to a climax.

However, Mr. Wiseguy was too wise to go against the tide of convention, so most of the time he carried books as conventional culture-decorations.

Vocationally, Mr. Wiseguy was too light for heavy work and too heavy for light work. So he practically never worked.

Politically, he was too stupid to be a Conservative and too wise to be a Communist. His being a Socialist was the policy of The Bureau of Exploitation. Since Mr. Thomas had become the favorite dish of Mr. Morgan and was passionately admired by General Pershing,[5] Mr. Wiseguy accepted the Bureau's suggestion wisely and executed the Bureau's policy swelly.

IF MISS DIGGER CAME

"A ten-cent check,
I had my coffee an'
I have only a nickel
In my hand."

Mr. Nut was worrying how he could get out of the cafeteria. He was worrying still more as to whether Miss Digger would come in, while he was a nickel short. That would be embarrassing.

After Miss Stubborn left the movie-house two years ago, Miss Digger wrote her many letters. She sent her many packages of chewing gum. And occasionally a pair of imitation-silk stockings.

Miss Digger wrote her that when she was her age, she had had the same bad temper and the same stubbornness. But one could not live by one's temper and stubbornness. This was a realistic world.

—What can a girl do? (Miss Digger wrote) This world has plenty of girls. And nowadays one seldom sees a pock-marked one or one with a harelip.

One way or another, each girl can be her own type.

A fat girl can be developed in a hot-baby style. There is a hot summer, a tropic sun, but there will also be a chilling winter night.

A skinny one can be developed by nature without any laborious reducing, or starving herself to death into a slender darling, who will be good in a Palm Beach, summer, moonlight evening.

If she is neither too fat nor too skinny, God's will made her good for the season of balmy Spring and days of gay Autumn.

Each type has its attraction and each style has its market.

For food, some like beef, some like fish, and some like pork. So in the field of women, also, there will be customers having every taste.

But the trouble is (Miss Digger wrote) that the number of customers who have Dough is rather limited. And according to the Law of Supply and Demand (which Miss Digger learned about in college and from her father's sermon in the church) there is strenuous competition.[6] And, still according to the theory of the struggle for existence, the first thing a girl needs to be conscious of is that she should get rid of her stubbornness, as part of a ceaseless effort towards adapting herself to her environment.

Miss Digger never received any reply. But she was satisfied with the fact that she had done her part in serving humanity.

While Miss Digger was working in the movie-house, every week she had a chance to see a free show.

Every time, after seeing a free show and before going to work in the little ticket-box, she faced the mirror in the ladies' room for a long, long time.

She looked at herself from head to foot and made a comparison between herself and the heroine in the show.

Miss Digger did not hate herself in the least.

Miss Digger had a square face, round at the end.

She had a pair of attractive blue eyes, with eyelashes grouped and waxed together by sevens or eights. These looked like circles of needles with their points up and down.

When the eyelids closed and separated, these moving needles gave the opposite sex a mysterious feeling of "Oh Baby!"

The eyelids were outlined with dark blue, which made the eyes look deeper and the eyebrows more striking.

Miss Digger's blond hair was permanently waved and combed back. That made her forehead large enough for four people to play a card game on.

Her lips were painted sufficiently to give a few dozen love-marks with no need of a further supply of lipstick.

Her teeth were still in the process of straightening; so they were carefully sealed to avoid their being seen.

Two would-be-insured, million-dollar legs were stockinged by a pair of brown fish-nets. And their arrow-lines shot up to whereabouts unknown.

Miss Digger examined her front.

The cut of her dress was so low that the roots of her breasts could be seen without a bending gesture. And the main parts of them were so prominent that they could give a dance-partner a tickling sensation. As the right-side one was comparatively better-developed, it showed that her boss, Mr. System, was a left-handed man.

Miss Digger turned and examined her back.

She noticed that her hips were God-given, too. She walked forward and backward a few steps. She was glad that they gave an assurance of comfort and richness of flexibility.

Miss Digger turned and faced the mirror again.

She complained a bit, because her boss, Mr. System, bit too hard and made a mark on an obvious spot.

Since she had so attractive a body and knew how to better it, some day, she would be in the same position as the heroine in the picture. "Oh, gee! That's grand! Swell!" she said to herself, in congratulation.

Where there is a will, there is a way, and finally Miss Digger got her man.

Miss Digger lived with her boss, Mr. System, weekendly.

The result was very good.

Miss Digger would work up a pint of spit and spit it forth on his small, fat, lazy, meaningless nose!

When her heart was full of hate, she sat and watched his behind move. As he walked, the fat flesh and the wrinkling of his trousers nauseated her.

And that elephantine hunk of purplish flesh and that wave of heat from his body were killing her.

Many times, Mr. System ground his teeth and in a guttural voice told her: "If you like to look at those young brats, why don't you go and sleep with them?"

Then he would suddenly come to her bed and expect her to turn like a dog on its back and enjoy his lustful maneuvers!

After five months of the Week-End Home Life, Miss Digger left Mr. System.

Miss Digger dug nothing out of Mr. System.

Now what could Miss Digger do?

Go to a Burlesque House to shake her breasts and move her hips?

She would not be as well-fitted for this as those who hadn't had a college education of four years. For such training was not given in college.

Should she hurry and get this training now?

She was twenty-five years of age. Too late.

Get a job in a business office?

She was not young enough to have a successful interview. And now—depression, and so many good-looking, young girls were out of jobs!

So Miss Digger could be seen along Fourteenth Street late at night, getting the fellows to go to speakeasies and spend money in them. She got commissions from the owners for this. . . . She had been engaged in this occupation three months ago, when Nut had met her, and while he was working.

VII:

"WORSE THAN A
CAPITALIST!"

*"A ten-cent check,
I had my coffee an'
I have only a nickel
In my hand."*

It was seven o'clock.
   Nut could not get out.
   And Mr. Nut was hungry.

He was looking outside and he saw a little boy making a face at him.
   "You little brat, mind your own business!" Nut muttered quickly.
   A few seconds later the boy came in and sat quietly on the opposite side of Nut's table.
   "Say, Comrade, how did you like the *Pioneer*⁷ you bought from me three months ago in our Party Cafeteria?" the boy whispered, with one eye on the manager and one eye on Mr. Nut.
   Now Mr. Nut remembered that he had met the boy before.
   "This new issue's good! Give me a nickel," the boy continued.
   Mr. Nut, with one eye on the manager and one eye on the boy, did not say anything.
   "Say, Comrade, this capitalist is no good. He chased me away from here yesterday. I didn't sell any here," the kid whispered to Nut.
   Mr. Nut, with one eye on the manager and one eye on the kid, said nothing.
   "Comrade, don't worry! I am ten. By the time I'm fifteen

this cafeteria will be ours.[8] No more capitalists. Won't that be nice?" the boy continued.

Mr. Nut, with one eye on the manager and one eye on the boy, still said nothing.

"You know? I sold nine copies yesterday. Give me a nickel. That'll make it ten!"

"No. I don't want it." Mr. Nut was getting mad. But he dared not make any noise.

"Why? I know. You aren't a Pioneer. You don't want this magazine! Have you children at home like me? Don't give them too much candy. Give them this magazine! Too much candy spoils their teeth. We need teeth to bite the Capitalists. This magazine makes the brain good. A good brain makes a good revolution!"

"No, I don't want it," Nut answered.

"If you have no children, this magazine is good for yourself. Really. The workers here in this cafeteria get very little, Comrade Stubborn told me. Exploitation! The boss is rich. More of his stores open every day! The workers aren't organized. They have men's heads, but children's brains! Buy this magazine. Only a nickel!"

Mr. Nut didn't like the kid. But he didn't know how to get rid of him. He just said: "Be a good boy. Next time I'll buy one."

"Say, Comrade, buy one now. The Revolution won't wait. You understand?"

Mr. Nut was worrying how he could get out of the place. Looking around, he saw he knew no one. He was hungry.

"Comrade, are you a Party member? What Unit?" the kid continued.

"Stop Comrading me. I am a Mister. Go away; I don't want to buy anything!" Nut was getting mad.

"We call Roosevelt 'Mister', Norman Thomas 'Mister', Trotsky 'Mister', and Lovestone 'Mister'.[9] I call you, Comrade. I am good to you. Give me a nickel. Buy a copy!"

Mr. Nut was mad. He didn't know how to answer the kid. He didn't know how to chase the kid away. He dared not raise his voice, for he was afraid of the manager. He had only one nickel for a ten-cent check. He was mad. He was mad as anything.

"Say, I only want your nickel," the kid said in a tone of surprise. "I don't want your life. I'll give you the magazine. You see, I know you."

"I have no change. You understand?"

"Haven't you a dollar bill? I can change it for you."

"No. I lost my purse."

"What! Where? Too bad. But you have a nickel?"

"I have only one nickel."

"If you don't live very far, give me your nickel and walk home. It's good exercise. Outside, fresh air. In demonstrations, I've walked many blocks."

Mr. Nut thought that this Russian Brat was more of a pest than a fellow who had sold him a copy of *China Red*.[10]

Nut was angry. But he was afraid of the manager and dared not raise his voice. So he just whispered and told his story. It was embarrassing.

"But I have a ten-cent check," he said to the boy.

"That's all right. You can't get out, anyhow. You call up your friends and ask them to send you some money, right now. Then you might find your purse home, maybe, or when you get your next pay, you can give back the money. I must go now, I can't wait. Give me the nickel. Here is the magazine! O.K?"

Mr. Nut was mad. He thought that Communists were more greedy than the so-called capitalists. And even this little Russian Brat knew how to suck his last nickel away, while he, Mr. Nut, was in such a condition.

Mr. Nut was mad. However he dared not become too mad. So he had to tell the kid the real story:

"I just lied, when I told you I lost my purse. I'm out of work for three months. I've no one I can borrow money from. I've a ten-cent check and a nickel in my pocket. I'm stuck here. So, my little Mister, I've told you everything. Now go away. I won't and can't buy your magazine. Be a good boy and go!"

"I Comrade you, don't I? You shouldn't Mister me. Why? So you're unemployed? Join the Unemployed Council![11] Fight for Unemployment Insurance! Get Unemployed Relief! Why!— This is a rich country!"

"All right. Now go away. Be a good boy," said Nut.

No, Mr. Nut would not join the Unemployed Council. That was Red. Russian Stuff! But Mr. Nut had to lie, so he could get rid of that Russian Brat. That was the second time that Nut had lied.

The kid didn't move. And he still sat there.

Mr. Nut was mad, mad as anything.

"Say, what's the matter now?" Nut asked angrily.

"Wait a minute. I haven't an application card of the Unemployed Council, but I've got to have your name and address. Say, do you know where the Unemployed Council is?" asked the kid.

Mr. Nut was mad, mad as anything. He didn't know the address of the Unemployed Council. And he didn't want to know it. But he didn't know how to get rid of the brat. So he had to lie again: "I know where it is! I know! Go away!"

"Give me your address, anyhow," said the kid.

"Mr. Nut, General Delivery, N. Y. City," Nut wrote down.

The kid took the paper Nut handed him. But he still sat there with his little hand scratching his hair, as if he were thinking.

And he finally told Mr. Nut: "I can help you."

"I don't take money from a kid. Now go!"

"No, I'm not giving you a nickel. This is magazine money. I have to turn it into my unit. But my father bought me a copy of the magazine. I've read it. I'll give you my copy. You sell it. You make a nickel. You pay the check. But watch the manager. If you have the time, look over the magazine before you sell it. It's good."

Mr. Nut would not have sold that copy even for a hundred dollars. But that Russian Brat was so good, and had wasted so much time on him. So Mr. Nut held his nickel in his hand and told the Russian brat: "Here is my nickel! A ten-cent check. A nickel in my pocket—I'm in Hell. Ten-cent check, nothing in my pocket. That isn't any worse. Nut's in Hell anyhow. A nickel doesn't make any difference to me."

"No, I won't take your last nickel. My mother told me not to do such a thing."

"No. I won't take a copy for nothing!"

"No, I won't take your last nickel."

"No, I won't take something for nothing." Mr. Nut put the nickel in the kid's pocket and pushed him away.

The kid threw the nickel back to the table, on top of the magazine, and ran away.

"Mr. Cashier:" the kid said, "I didn't buy anything; here is the check!"

The Russian Brat was happy. He had got a member for the Unemployed Council.

VIII:

WITH ONE GLASS
OF WATER

"A ten-cent check,
I had my coffee an'
I have only a nickel
In my hand."

About nine o'clock, a fellow was passing outside with a cane hanging on his left arm, gloves in his left hand. His derby was tilted on his head. His right hand was making a sound with its fingers. All this gave him a perfect gaiety; a leisurely, gentlemanly grandeur.

Yes, it was Mr. Wiseguy.

Mr. Nut lifted high the magazine which the boy had left for him.

This brought no result.

Then Nut went to the front and tapped at the window.

Wiseguy saw him, pushed the revolving door, took a check and joined Mr. Nut.

"How do you do, my dear friend Mr. Nut?" Mr. Wiseguy smiled with his face-muscles lifted and a mouth-closed smile when he saluted Mr. Nut. "Where have you been? I haven't seen you for ages, old fellow. Are you working? Are you making money? How is the world treating you?"

Nut went to his seat and made a gesture to ask Mr. Wiseguy to sit on the other side of the table.

"I'd like to face the outside. Would you mind if I sat beside you?" said Mr. Wiseguy.

"Why not? Sure," said Mr. Nut. He knew that Mr. Wiseguy wanted to look at the girls.

Everything was settled.

Mr. Nut moved his lips a little and said nothing.

"Mr. Nut, are you growing a beard, too, to imitate me? A beard alone won't make you wise. Say, I had better sell you my brain. How much can you offer?"

Mr. Nut moved his lips a little but didn't say anything.

"What makes you so quiet? I know. It is Miss Digger who's bothering you. It's more than three months already and you haven't forgot her yet. Do you remember the Four F Theory regarding the technique of handling a woman? The last principle of the four, you know, is Forget. If you've gone through the Third, you should forget. Because you've already had what you wanted. In other words, you've got your money's worth. If you haven't experienced the Third Principle, you should forget also. Because maybe your management of the Second Principle was not so good. Maybe you didn't know how to fool her. Sometimes, money alone won't work. The thing to do now is to find another girl."

Mr. Nut was hungry. He wished that Mr. Wiseguy would ask him to have something. Having heard Mr. Wiseguy "nut" him, he had to open his mouth himself: "You know, Mr. Wiseguy . . ."

"I know what!" Mr. Wiseguy interrupted. "You mean you've found a new one. Or do you mean that you have got what you wanted from Miss Digger? Say, don't bluff me. I'm a wiseguy. Say, be a friend of mine, won't you? Tell me where Miss Digger is. I'll go with you. I wouldn't double-cross you, Mr. Nut. I've got plenty of girls."

"You know, my friend, Mr. Wiseguy, I'm in some trouble."

"What's the trouble? I know. I am a wiseguy. You're afraid that I will spend your money. No. Though I, Mr. Wiseguy, have done lots of services for others, I'll never ask for a reward."

"No. No. . . ." said Mr. Nut.

"For instance, once we went to a restaurant together and I didn't ask you to pay the bill. It was the waiter who gave you the check. Another time we went to a speakeasy and I didn't ask you to pay. It was when I went to the washroom that you paid the check. Can you tell me that when I go out with you, I shouldn't go to the washroom? Another time I misplaced my purse. I told you that you should hold the check for a while. You were in a hurry, and you paid it. Whose fault was that? Even in a small matter like carfare, you always took advantage of the time when my shoelaces were loose and put a nickel in the slot for me. Could I take your nickel out of the slot?"

Mr. Nut didn't hear clearly what he said. But he noticed that the face of Mr. Wiseguy had become very serious. For heaven's sake! How could he get a nickel from him. Mr. Nut was hungry. But he said merely: "No, that isn't my trouble at all."

"I am a wiseguy. I can study your mind. You always smile. And today . . . See I know . . . Here is my purse. You see! What is in it? What color is the bill? I have plenty of bills. Now—you get me?"

When Mr. Nut saw the dollar bills in Mr. Wiseguy's billfold, he could not control himself any longer and poured everything out. "Mr. Wiseguy! I am sorry. I pawned everything at the pawnshop that the Uncle would take. I came here at two o'clock this afternoon. I had coffee and doughnuts. For I had one dime and a nickel, when I came in. Later, I searched and searched and I could not find my dime. I have been here about seven hours. I haven't eaten anything since those dough nuts. I'd like to borrow a dollar from you. Maybe I can find a job tomorrow. Then I'll pay you back. You've known me for about a year. Can't you trust me?"

Mr. Wiseguy was listening. He felt that the city he was in was no longer New York City. The month was no longer April. He felt as if he were in Little America, by the South Pole; he was being chilled. His blood was freezing. His fingers were trembling. He would have liked to stop Mr. Nut from pouring out his sad stories. But his breath was so short, he could not raise his voice high enough to make Mr. Nut hear. Finally he said: "Are you kidding me?"

"No, I never told a lie in all my life," answered Mr. Nut.

(No.—He had lied three times to the Russian Brat.)

"This is the first time in my life that I incorrectly estimated a situation." Wiseguy spoke to himself; then he turned to Mr. Nut:

"By the way, I've been here for twenty minutes and I haven't got anything yet. So excuse me just a minute. Do you want anything?"

Mr. Wiseguy left.
  Mr. Wiseguy returned.
  With one glass of water!

IX:

A FEELING OF NOT ENOUGH

"A ten-cent check,
I had my coffee an'
I have only a nickel
In my hand."

It was ten o'clock.

Nut could not go out of the cafeteria.

And he was starving in the cafeteria.

Miss Digger was passing outside of the cafeteria.

She had met Mr. Nut three months ago in this very cafeteria.

They had walked arm in arm, to a speakeasy on Second Avenue and Twelfth Street.

No, Miss Digger didn't tell Mr. Nut that they were going to a speakeasy. She knew Mr. Nut might be afraid and refuse to go. For in days like these, how could a plain workman afford to go to speakeasies.

She had just told him she was thirsty and would like to go somewhere to have a glass of beer. For fifty cents they could get a large pitcher of it. And that pitcher would last for hours. Then they could have the place to talk in. To talk over many things! It was January, then. The weather was too cold to stroll on Fifth Avenue.

For Mr. Nut, it was the first time he had with him a girl who was so friendly. And she was a beautiful girl. Nut was very happy.

While they were walking along Fourteenth Street, down Fourth Avenue and then to the left, Mr. Nut felt that his arm was heavily insulated by his coat and overcoat and also the coat and dress of Miss Digger. Nevertheless, he felt that a certain part of the muscle of Miss Digger along the upper part of her arm was soft, tender and warm. And such a softness, tenderness and warmth gave him a feeling of not enough.

He put his arm a little lower and so made the back of his hand touch the very part underneath it. That meant that Mr. Nut was one coat and one overcoat nearer to her. He felt better. Meantime Miss Digger didn't protest. She held the hand of Mr. Nut tighter. To Mr. Nut that meant: "You are heartily welcome."

As they were walking on, Mr. Nut again had a feeling of not enough. Miss Digger pushed his hand away with her hand and murmured: "Stop! Please don't!" Mr. Nut understood that she meant: "Please do not stop." So he stretched his arm across her back and placed his hand under her shoulder, almost as if they were automobile riding. For a few minutes, everything was quiet. Mr. Nut was enjoying it.

A few minutes more, and Mr. Nut again had the feeling of not enough. He stopped walking. He asked for a kiss and tried to take one. Miss Digger turned her head away and told him that he was in too much of a hurry.

Mr. Nut didn't say anything. They began to walk again.

A few minutes later, Mr. Nut again stopped. This time he didn't ask. He just kissed her. This time Miss Digger didn't say anything in protest, either.

So they kissed. They kissed in just a movie style.

Mr. Nut was smiling. For he felt better.

A few minutes later, Mr. Nut stopped again.

Miss Digger looked at him and was wondering what he was going to ask. Nut told her he wanted a real kiss in a true, realistic, progressive, wet way. Miss Digger knew what he meant and said coyly: "There's plenty of time yet."

Mr. Nut began to realize that he was too greedy. And that he had got more than what he had paid for. That Miss Digger's twenty-cent check in the cafeteria.

"By the way, may I inquire what is your definition of a kiss?" highbrowed Mr. Nut.

Miss Digger was stuck.

Then he dug a piece of paper from his hip-pocket and read this to Miss Digger under the street-light:

"A kiss is a peculiar proposition:

Of no use to one,

Bliss to two:

The small boy gets it for nothing,

The young man has to steal it,

And the old man has to buy it:

To a young girl it means cash-Out,

To an old maid it means cash-In."[12]

"Say, it's an old story, but why should you be sarcastic," asked Miss Digger.

"No. No. I am now—what shall I say—very romantic," answered Nut.

Finally they reached the beer-place.

They sat down. A waiter came and mentioned all those fancy names. Mr. Nut ordered: "Beer! Nothing but beer! Beer for fifty cents! No more! No less!"

As the beer began to be poured from the pitcher to the glass, he thought that they had had the first act of a romance on the way to this place. Now the second act had just begun. And the third act was yet to come.

He moved the glass to Miss Digger. Then he filled his own glass. They drank together.

While they were drinking Mr. Nut was figuring. Twenty cents he had paid in the cafeteria. Now fifty cents for the beer. And a few cents more for a tip. The whole evening would not cost him more than a dollar. He would still have eleven dollars left. He would still have money for his rent, laundry and the expenses of the rest of the week. He was safe.

When Miss Digger finished the glass, she told Mr. Nut that the beer was all too light for her and if he didn't mind she would like to have a glass of mixed drinks. Yes, Mr. Nut did mind. But Mr. Nut could not afford to say so.

He thought that one glass of mixed drinks might cost him just another fifty cents more. And that he would still have ten dollars and fifty cents left.

Nut ordered the mixed drinks for Miss Digger. He stuck to beer himself.

Miss Digger finished the mixed drinks. She flattered Nut a little, and asked for another glass—got it and drank it. But Nut could not understand how she could finish those two glasses so easily, easier than he did his beer.

Suddenly Miss Digger looked drunk, rang the table bell drunkenly and without asking Mr. Nut, ordered one glass after another. Now Mr. Nut had to tell her that he had only eleven dollars. He did tell her.

Miss Digger, on hearing this, suddenly changed her face and said to him:

"So you tell me you have only eleven dollars. Why don't you tell me the real reason. The real reason is that you're a piker[13] and a cheap one, the kind that doesn't want to spend one rusty penny on a girl! You don't deserve to go with any girl, you cheapskate, you! I hope you'll have enough money to go with others! You'll get yours! You haven't got hold of the right party yet! And when you do, God pity you . . ."

The check was coming. Exactly eleven dollars.

That was the story of what had happened to Mr. Nut three months ago, while he was working.

Tonight Miss Digger entered the cafeteria again.

Miss Digger took a seat at the table of Mr. Nut and Mr. Wiseguy.

Mr. Nut saw Miss Digger entering and sitting at his table. She sat opposite to Mr. Nut and just opposite to Mr. Wiseguy.

But Mr. Nut no longer had the feeling of not enough.

X:

OUT IN A
NO-WAY-OUT WAY

"A ten-cent check,
I had my coffee an'
I have only a nickel
In my hand."

It was a quarter to eleven. A Scottsboro Defense meeting in Irving Plaza had just adjourned.[14] Communists and sympathizers, a whole crowd, passed by the window. Many went home directly. Many came into the cafeteria and Comrade Stubborn was one of the people who came in.

Stubborn noticed and was interested in Mr. Nut right away. When she had met him in the Party cafeteria to get a contribution from him, he had been bourgeois-looking. Now he seemed much more proletarian. And he had a Communist Children's Magazine. What progress in a period of three months!

She moved to the empty seat just across from Mr. Nut.

She didn't talk to Mr. Nut right away. She acted as if she could not get any other seat and that therefore she had to sit there.

Mr. Nut knew that this girl whom he had met twice, three months ago in the Communist cafeteria, was coming again to sell him some propaganda stuff. Since that Russian Brat had caused him enough trouble already early that evening, he had to be careful this time. So he held the Communist Children's Magazine high in order to hide from Stubborn.

Miss Digger looked at Stubborn attentively as if she had met her somewhere before.

She looked.

She looked.

Finally Miss Digger asked:

"Are you the girl who two years ago worked in the same movie-house where I worked? Didn't you, two weeks after you came, slap the boss, Mr. System, and leave? Tell me, are you Stubborn?"

"Yes. Stubborn is my name."

"For heaven's sake! Oh, gee! I am so glad to see you again. I'm Miss Digger. I knew you had become a Communist. But I never saw you here before. I am so glad. Oh, gee! Life in New York is so funny. Coming together and separating are so uncertain. Oh, what a machine age!"[15]

"Miss Digger, I'm so glad to see you," answered Stubborn.

"What has become of your professor-back? How did you straighten that out, Stubborn?" Miss Digger used her hand to feel Stubborn's back, who was sitting beside her.

"If I can't straighten out a professor-back, how am I going to straighten out this crooked world?"

"That is great. Sounds heroic. Oh, gee!" commented Miss Digger jokingly.

"I'm sorry. I meant how are *we* going to straighten out this crooked world," added Stubborn apologetically.

"That's right! We . . . the people . . ." Mr. Wiseguy interrupted with his Oxford and Harvard accent.

"No, I mean we, the WORKERS, are going to straighten out this crooked world," said Stubborn scientifically.

"Don't you see I am a Socialist. Here is the *New Leader*,[16] our paper."

"No, I would not read that yellow sheet," replied Stubborn, revolutionarily.

"That is the trouble with you Communists. You're so fanatic!" said Mr. Wiseguy.

"Say, Mister," demanded Stubborn, "Can't you cut out that Oxford and Harvard accent. It hurts me."

"That is the trouble with you radicals. You fight too much among yourselves. If you so-called workers stopped hitting one another and worked together, maybe, some day, you'd get somewhere," remarked Miss Digger, compromisingly and broad-mindedly.

At this moment Mr. Wiseguy thought that now his opportunity had come to show his generosity in the presence of two girls. So he opened his leather billfold and took a nickel out of it and told Mr. Nut: "Here is a nickel, which I'd like to give you. Now you have ten cents in your pocket and ten cents on your check. You can go out. And get some fresh air outside. It's not a loan. I am running no bank. I just give it to you."

Oh, boy, how much prestige this nickel might bring to him— Mr. Wiseguy.

Hearing this, Mr. Nut suddenly became Nut-like and exclaimed to Mr. Wiseguy: "This won't do. If you don't want to give me a dollar, don't give me a nickel. I want no charity. I want a loan. I am no bum. I am just a worker who is out of a job. That is all! You know how damn little you've spent on me before this. And Miss Digger, you should take off that sarcastic smile. You know why!"

"That's O.K. to me! That saves me a nickel. A nickel is five cents." Mr. Wiseguy took the nickel back, looked at it, at Miss Digger and said to himself: "It served the purpose."

"Say, Comrade," said Stubborn, "you contributed twenty-five cents for the Scottsboro Defense Fund in the Party Cafeteria. I can help you to a nickel. I wish I had more."

"You helped black people, now black people help you," said a Negro, who had been selling a Communist paper outside and had come in for coffee.

"Say, Comrade, if you are out of work, why don't you join the Unemployed Council?" Stubborn said again, while she was handing Mr. Nut the nickel.

"I, Nut, will take no money from a girl. I'll take no money from a Red. I won't sell my Flag for five cents. I will take no money from a black man. I won't disgrace the white race! I'm just out of work and just happened to lose my dime. I won't pay the check. Send the check to Wall Street. Send the check to

J. P. Morgan![17] What can the boss of this cafeteria do? Call the police? I'll go to the Police Station! That's O.K. I've got no place to go to, anyhow!"

When Mr. Nut began making noise, the boss, Mr. System, signaled with his eyes to the gangster and the dicks[18] who were inside of the cafeteria, to give Mr. Nut a few punches right away.

Two policemen came in. They took Nut outside and hit him just in front of the window-glass of the cafeteria, so that the patrons inside could see what happened. This prevented Nut's blood from soiling the cafeteria floor and at the same time warned others what would happen if they did not pay their checks.

Some who went outside to help Mr. Nut were clubbed also. Among them were Stubborn, a Negro and a worker in that very cafeteria.

The worker, besides, lost his job next day, because he had minded somebody else's business.

A few curious spectators also got hurt, accidentally.

Mr. Nut now began to realize that the policeman's Irish club clubbed his very Anglo-Saxon, Teutonic and Yankee head the same as other heads.

And the blood of the colored race and the blood of the white race that fell on the cement pavement were of one color.

Nut realized also that Communists were not necessarily bad people who started trouble and then stepped to a safety zone and let other fellows take the consequences.

Thus Mr. Nut got out—out in a no-way-out way.

ACT II

XI:

HE WAS POETIZING

. . . Heaven is above,
  Hell below.
  Things give heat,
  Things keep warmth.
  Packed warehouse,
  Crowded shop window.
  Nothing in pocket,
  Where to go?

Heaven is above,
  Hell below.
  Plenty of wheat,
  Plenty of cotton.
  Rich men's joy,
  Farmers' woe.
  Nothing in pocket,
  Where to go?

Heaven is above,
  Hell below.
  Street links with avenue,
  Avenue links with highway,
  Leads near! Leads far!
  Buffalo,
  Chicago,
  San Diego.
  Nothing in pocket,
  Where to go?

Heaven is above,
    Hell below.
    Rich men are yachting,
    To and fro.
    Nothing in pocket,
    Where to go?

Heaven is above,
    Hell below.
    Apartment high,
    Apartment low.
    Nothing in pocket,
    Where to go?

Heaven is above,
    Hell below.
    Your parrot's a pet,
    And it can speak—
    And I can smile.
    Let me share its room!
    A dog's a pet
    That can stand up
    As stands a man.
    But *always* I
    Walk like a man.
    Let me share its home!
    Nothing in pocket,
    Where to go?

Heaven is above,
    Hell below.
    Fiddles are played
    By blind men who
    For pennies beg
    In city streets.
    God in Heaven,

Take out my eyes.
With eyes I can see.
Nothing in pocket,
Where to go?

Heaven is above,
   Hell below.
   Pencils are sold
   By cripples who
   For pennies beg
   In city streets.
   God in Heaven,
   Chop off my legs!
   With legs I can walk.
   Nothing in pocket,
   Where to go?

Heaven is above,
   Hell below.
   Mother, sent me out
   Of your womb.
   Now please take me back
   Into your tomb!
   Nothing in pocket,
   Where to go?

Heaven is above,
   Hell below.
   You earthquake,
   You volcano,
   Come near!
   Come soon!
   Nothing in pocket,
   Where to go?

It's under this system!
   It's under this system!

Mr. System
  Beware:
  The Hanging
  On
  Union Square! . . .

XII:

BEFORE THE ARRIVAL
OF AN AMBULANCE

"Heaven is above,
Hell below.
Nothing in pocket,
Where to go?"

It was Mr. Nut poetizing.

One o'clock.

At the corner of Fourteenth Street and First Avenue, Mr. Nut
saw a garbage-can standing in front of another cafeteria.
    He stopped.
    He looked in.
    He put his right hand in.
    To see if there was anything inside.
    An old man came running towards him. He yelled:
    "Get away from here! This is my station. I've got a sick wife
to feed. You're a young fellow: why don't you go to the Relief
Building?[1] You have the strength. They have to feed you! They
are afraid that you will make trouble."
    The old man covered the garbage-can with his whole body
to keep it from Mr. Nut. Picking! Eating! And murmuring!
    Nut moved to the other side of the can.
    "Don't touch this can!" continued the old man. "This is my
station!"
    "What do you mean," asked Nut, "your station?"
    "You heard me! Can't you understand English? I have been
living by this can for three months now."
    Nut moved back a few steps. Still looking on.

The snow whitened the pavement.

And the melting snow washed away all the dirt from the old man's bony hands. They were as pale and bloodless as wax.

While the old man kept on digging, a tin box of Drainpipe Solvent appeared, alongside of a piece of rotten apple-pie. The old man picked up the pie with joy, and was ready to swallow it.

Nut dashed forward and grabbed the old man's hand. He dropped the pie on the ground.

"You bastard! You take the food from an old man's mouth! You damned hero!"

"Now look here. This pie, with that white powder on, is poison! It can put your stomach and lungs out of commission. It will kill you!"

"Is that so?" said the disappointed old man. "Now you, young fellow, you have spoiled my opportunity. I'm sick. I'm tired. I'm a coward and can't kill myself. I've prayed that some day I will die just in the way you tell me, and so get rid of my misery. Now you have delayed my voyage to Heaven."

Nut was hungry.

Nut had to move.

He went back to Third Avenue and from Fourteenth Street he followed the Third Avenue Elevated towards downtown.

He reached Thirteenth Street.

A half-drunk and half-awake bum approached him and asked for a cigarette.

"Who the hell wants to work?" the fellow began talking. "I ain't no sap. It's snowing so I'll have good business tomorrow. I'll make lots of nickels and pennies! Who wants to work? The big shots do nothing but enjoy everything. They drink champagne, I drink wood alcohol! Poison. They are yachting! Me? Around Third Avenue! Tell me, ain't that justice? For heaven's sake, give me a cigarette!"

Nut had no cigarette to give.

He walked from Twelfth Street to Eleventh.

A middle-aged fellow with a Southern accent approached

Nut and asked him if he could spare a penny so that he would have thirty-five cents with which to go to a cheap hotel on the Bowery.[2] He was a farmer. He had come from the South to this city and tried to find a job here. And he hadn't slept for two nights. He already had thirty-four cents.

Nut had no penny to spare.

Nut walked on from Eleventh Street to Tenth Street.

Another fellow came to him and asked him if he had a match.

Mr. Nut stopped. Searched.

In addition to a match, which Nut gave to the fellow, he felt something small, round and solid in the corner of his vest-pocket.

Before using his eyes to see it, Nut prayed: "Let it not be a button. I have lots of buttons. Let it be a dime."

If it were a dime, Nut would be able to have a bowl of soup together with a piece of butter, and two Big, Big Rolls!

For Heaven's sake! It was a penny.

Nut went back a block.

He found the Southern fellow standing there, shivering.

"I've just found a penny in my pocket. Take it and go to sleep."

"Thanks a lot," the fellow smiled gratefully.

"Don't mention it. One penny will do me no good anyhow."

"God bless J. P. Morgan," said the Southern fellow, "last year he made a speech on the radio. This is real Block Aid!"[3]

Snow was falling, heavier and heavier.

Snow was falling, faster and faster.

Nut followed the Third Avenue El again, walking back in the downtown direction.

He saw a woman about fifty who walked as if one of her legs were long and one short.

She called out to him:

"Say, whaddaya say?"

Nut had nothing to say.

At the corner of Ninth Street, he turned west to Fourth Avenue.

On his way he saw many people crowded in a hallway. At the place where the street was darker, he saw many people lying on the stone floors of a hallway. They were covered with newspapers and were sleeping.

Nut walked and walked.

He reached Washington Square and Fifth Avenue.

He saw a fellow rather well-dressed, lying on the sidewalk.

His body was stiff, the two legs straight, the two feet parted. The two hands coming from his overcoat sleeves had their palms upward. His face was half-covered with his hat. His mouth was open. The man wasn't breathing. His body was very stiff.

"Complete, dignified funeral for $150, with ornamented casket. As inexpensive as required and as impressive as desired."

Nut would like to know, Who, how, and why? A policeman stood nearby and smiled at him and said icily, "Starvation! Take a walk, it's none of your business! Or I'll hang you!"

For, if Nut remained before the arrival of an ambulance there wouldn't be enough time for the cop to pick something out of the starved, unemployed man's pocket.

XIII:

A WILLOW IN A WINDY SPRING

"Heaven is above,
Hell below.
Nothing in pocket.
Where to go?"

It was two o'clock.
  Nut moved on.

Near the corner of Eighth Street and Sixth Avenue, there was a young fellow with long hair and no hat on. His hair was different from that of the men on Third Avenue. It was long but it was richly oiled and it was carefully scissored along his neck. And the muffler which he took out from a pocket of his overcoat was beautifully colored. His eyebrows were poetically arranged, and they resembled those of Miss Digger. Whether his face was powdered or was just affected by the street light, Nut could not tell. But he could tell that the lips of that young fellow were painted and his tongue went out just a little bit and made his tiny mouth more noticeable. As he walked, his body waved to and fro, his hips swayed left and right. It reminded Nut of a willow in a windy spring.

"Haven't we met somewhere before? Oh, gracious, I am so glad to see you again. And this is just the moment!" said the young fellow, welcomingly. He looked at Mr. Nut very pleasedly, and one of his hands had already been put under the arm of Mr. Nut.
  "I never saw you before. You are mistaken," said Mr. Nut coldly.

"Oh, what's the difference? Strangers this time. Acquaintances next time."

Another fellow with some papers under his arm touched the young fellow's back and said: "Remember that sailor last winter?" Then he ran away.

"The snow is terrible," said the handsome young fellow. "Let us go to my studio. We'll have a few drinks and then I'll read you a few of my poems."

Nut was pleased, for, in this world, there was still someone who had a good heart.

He followed the young fellow. They turned this way and that way. Walked on many crooked streets. Finally, they reached a building. One flight up. Two flights up. And then they came to a flat on the top floor. It had two rooms, with a kitchenette and a bathroom.

A large bed was alongside of the wall. There was a table near the window with a portable typewriter on it. And on the typewriter was a white sheet with a few short, uneven lines written on it. There were book-shelves, packed with books. On the wall there were a few pictures of men without any clothes on.

"Won't you have a seat?" asked the young fellow.

Nut was looking on.

"Please take that sofa. It's more comfortable."

Nut was seated. He was hungry, but not cold any more. The room had steam heat.

"By the way, do you know where the washroom is?"

"Thanks," answered Nut. He looked into the kitchenette.

"Excuse me just a minute." The young fellow went into the washroom and closed the door.

The young fellow came out, with his hair rearranged and his tongue going delicately to his lips. He had a small pocket-mirror in his hand.

"For goodness sake, take your hat and coat off. You will catch cold!"

"How do you like my studio? Isn't it nice and cute?"

"Indeed, a very nice flat," answered Nut.

"Say, don't say flat. It isn't poetic. It is a studio."

Nut was looking into the kitchenette.

The young fellow was looking at him.

The young fellow was neither looking at his head, nor at his feet. But at some place between both. That place was just midway between Nut's head and feet.

Nut didn't care where the young fellow looked at him. Nut was wondering where there was some food in the flat.

The young fellow saw the wondering in Mr. Nut's eyes, and politely said: "I beg your pardon. I promised to read you some poetry, didn't I?"

"No, thanks, I never liked poetry. I cannot understand it."

"Because it is not understandable, that is why it is poetry. If you could understand it, then it wouldn't be poetry anymore. If you want to read something as plain as Autumn air, you should go to Union Square and read some of their propaganda stuff."[4]

"Haven't you anything in your kitchenette?"

"Oh, I beg your pardon!"

The young fellow went into the kitchenette and brought out two small glasses, a bottle of gin and a package of sliced bread.

He poured one glass for Mr. Nut and one for himself.

"I don't drink," Mr. Nut said. "Please hand me that bread."

It was two o'clock on Sunday afternoon when Nut had had his "coffee and." Now it was thirty minutes past two, Monday morning.

Nut picked up two pieces, rolled them together and stuck them into his mouth. He turned his head toward the wall, and chewed them. They took too long to chew—so he just swallowed them. They stuck at the food passage and could not get in. Tears filled his eyes.

Then he took a glass of gin and poured it into his mouth. The gin greased the bread. He breathed. He coughed.

Nut took two more pieces of bread. And more and more. He finished the whole package.

Nut felt better. Much better. He wasn't hungry any more.

Nut stood up and ran his hands up and down his chest, to help his stomach get things straightened out. Then he stretched his hands and had a little exercise. And he left the sofa and had a little walk. He went into the washroom and had a few glasses of cold water. Then everything was all right. He was a new man. He began to smile. He thanked God for his daily bread. He felt that in this world there was a certain person who had a good heart.

While Nut was eating, drinking, walking, the young fellow was standing alongside of a table looking at a picture of a middle-aged woman. It was inscribed: "To my dear son—from his lonely and affectionate mother."

The air in the room made Nut sleepy. He lay on the sofa with his legs stretched out and his body relaxed. He slept.

As he lay sleeping, the young fellow sat on the arm of the sofa, and was running his hand through Mr. Nut's hair. The young fellow kissed Nut's forehead, cheeks and lips.

And because of the touching and kissing, and because of the strong perfume of that young fellow, Mr. Nut awoke.

The young fellow looked at him with his eyes mysteriously half-closed. He did not say a word.

Nut felt that something was wrong.

He stood up. Put on his hat and overcoat.

"Thanks a lot for your bread."

The young poet was disappointed and finally sang:

> "I wish your taste would be like mine—
> We could just be sixty-nine."

Nut opened the door, left the apartment and came out into the open.

XIV:

ARTIST AND UNIFORM

"Heaven is above,
Hell below.
Nothing in pocket,
Where to go?"

It was three o'clock.

Nut walked to where there was more light. He came to a big, big cafeteria near the subway station.

A small, old man paid his nickel check and came out.

"Why don't you go inside?" asked the old man.

"I'd better not, thanks."

"Have a cigarette?" The old man offered him a cigarette together with a charming smile.

"No, thanks."

"Isn't it beautiful to see the whole universe dressed in white?"

Nut said nothing.

"To get away from the artistic, and to say something humanistically," said the old man, "tomorrow there will be enough jobs for ten or twenty thousand unemployed men. And another chance for Tammany Hall politicians to get some graft."[5]

Nut was suddenly relieved when he heard the word "job." And he remarked to the old man: "Thanks a great deal for reminding me. Tomorrow I'll have a chance to get work and then I'll have a place to sleep."

"What! You mean you have no place to sleep tonight! Come along with me. I am a humanist and I think I can put you up just for tonight. Come on."

Because of the experience Nut had had with that young fellow about an hour ago, he was suspicious. He looked at the old man carefully. The old man was all right. For he had no powder on his face and no lipstick on his lips. And his small beard gave him a certain kind of dignity and the appearance of a professor. And as he walked his head bent forward a little. And his hips were steady—not dancing, as those of the young fellow were.

Nut thought: "As a matter of fact, you can never trust young fellows in a matter of that sort, but you can trust an old man."

"Thanks, Professor," Mr. Nut said to the old man. The professor walked fast. Nut followed.

They walked this way and turned that way. They reached their destination.

It was neither a flat nor as that young fellow called his place, a studio. It was just a furnished room in a rooming house. The room was a very small one on the top floor.

There was only one bed. On the dresser some magazines and books were piled up. On the floor there was another pile of old books and magazines. On the chair was an ashtray, a tooth brush and a few letters from newspapers. An alarm-clock was placed on the bed near the pillow.

The old man took off his worn-out, thin overcoat, and his shapeless dirty hat. He was breathless and was coughing.

Nut wondered: How could so small a room accommodate two persons?

"Want the washroom? Outside, turn left. But be quiet."

Nut went to wash, still wondering.

When Nut came back, the old man was pulling the window-shade down.

"Is this your room?" asked Mr. Nut.

"Why? Too small? In winter, the small ones are warmer!"

"But how can there be room for me, too?" inquired Nut.

"Oh, yeah . . ." the old man had changed the color of his face and answered sarcastically, "maybe you'd be comfortable on Park Avenue. The rich men keep their Park Avenue apartments empty, while they themselves are wintering in Florida. You still aren't too late, you know?"

Nut was ashamed of himself because of his question and decided to be content.

Nut took off his hat and overcoat.

But he was still wondering how he was going to find room to sleep.

"Don't hesitate! If you can get as big a room in Moscow for a whole family, you are lucky. In Moscow, to show that I was a writer and entitled even to a small room, I'd have to put on a uniform. Moscow, 'Artist in Uniform!'" "remarks the old man in a triumphant tone, somewhat Max-Eastman-ly.[6]

Nut untied his necktie.

The old man was coughing.

"Mr. Professor, thank you very much for everything." Nut finally got an idea and said to the old man: "Suppose you sleep on the bed. I'll lie on the floor. And if you don't mind, let me have your overcoat to cover myself. It's half-past three, anyhow."

"No, not that way. You are my guest."

"But you are older than I am."

"Nothing doing! As long as you're in my place, you are my guest!"

Nut said to himself: "There is still a gentleman in a world like this. This is civilization."

The old man was coughing.

"Thanks a great deal. Let's both sleep on the bed," Nut said with a smile, for he thought that he had just made a new discovery.

"Of course. You go inside. I'll sleep outside. I cough badly."

They lay down.

"Say, why don't you take those off. They are wet as hell," murmured the old man.

This was true. The trousers were wet since Nut had walked for almost three hours in the snowy night.

Nut took off his trousers.

The light was out.
Nut slept.

When he had slept for about ten or fifteen minutes, he felt the old man's hand touching his shoulder, back and then his waist.

Nut could not sleep. For the old man's touch was ticklish.

"Please cut that out," Nut told the old man, "or I'll get up and leave."

When the old man heard the word "leave" he stopped.

They slept.

A few minutes later, Nut again felt something uncomfortable touching the lower part of his back. It was not the old man's hand. Nor was it the old man's finger. Of course, Mr. Nut knew what it was. He turned on his back.

Now the old man's hand became active again. Nut couldn't stand it anymore. He jumped out of the bed. He put the light on.

"Now look here. This room is worth thirty-five cents in a cheap hotel on the Bowery. So I owe you seventeen and a half cents. Do you think seventeen and a half cents enough to make me a male prostitute?"

The old man looked ashamed of himself and then he became serious and said to Mr. Nut: "Listen, you are too materialistic, too commercial. And you have no artistic sense. I am not prostituting you. If you like, do whatever you wish with me. I review books. They paid me very little before. Now there is a depression, so there are fewer books and they pay me only with review copies. Tell me how I can help getting excited, when I read those sexy, hot novels. And how can I get the money to buy women and to cool myself? I tried to help myself sometimes. Jesus! That was so meaningless. Then I took whatever I could and it got to be a habit. Oh, Jesus! The Decline of the West!"

Nut didn't know what the professor was philosophizing about. He got dressed.

"The Decision of the Hour!"[7] the professor reminded Mr. Nut again.

Nut opened the door, went out of the rooming house and again out into the street.

XV:

SADISTIC OR CAPITALISTIC

"Heaven is above,
Hell below.
Nothing in pocket,
Where to go?"

It was four o'clock.

Again, Nut reached the big, big cafeteria, near the subway station.

Nut stood in front of the cafeteria and looked in.

A long, big, beautiful and expensive car came along the broad street, thick with snow. The car gave forth a musical sound.

The car stopped in front of the cafeteria and a husky fellow got out.

"Hello, chief! You are rather late tonight," said a bushy-haired, stockingless girl to the husky fellow as she came out of the cafeteria.

"I am not interested in chicken tonight. I am going to catch a rabbit. On a snowy night, there must be plenty around. Variety is the spice of life, you know!" said the husky fellow, half jokingly, half seriously.

He sat at a corner table, enthroned.

Partly because of curiosity, and partly because of necessity, Nut walked into the cafeteria, approached the husky fellow's table and asked politely: "May I ask, Sir, where the rabbits are? If you need any help I would like to go with you. I am out of work. Thirty-five cents an hour will satisfy me. I am not sure whether I can get a job shoveling snow tomorrow."

"Sit down!" commanded the Husky Fellow.

"No, thanks. I am just asking if you can give me a job. If you can't, I'll have to go out of the cafeteria right away."

"I asked you to sit down. Do as I tell you."

"Thank God." Nut sat down and thought, "This means that I'll have a job that will combine work and pleasure."

"What do you want to eat?" asked the husky fellow.

"Nothing, thanks," answered Nut.

"Do you mean that I can't pay your check?" the husky fellow asked angrily.

"No, Sir. I just had something," replied Nut.

"It's twenty-seven minutes . . . let me see . . . and twenty-five seconds past four! We've gotta go." The husky fellow looked at his wristwatch as he spoke.

He rose and left half a dollar on the table as a tip.

"A rich guy!" Nut said to himself.

"May I know your name?" asked Mr. Nut.

"Alphonse, alias Alphonse Brown, alias Al Scarface, alias Toothbrush-Mustache, alias Kingfish, alias Number 40886. You can just call me Mr. Ratsky."[8]

So Mr. Ratsky walked in front. Nut followed.

Mr. Ratsky paid the check.

The cashier and bouncer bowed to him again.

"You get in back. I'll drive," Nut was told.

Mr. Ratsky opened the door for Nut and Nut got in.

Since the car was big and heavy it ran smoothly, without shaking or jumping.

Nut didn't know where they were going. A few minutes later, the car stopped. Mr. Ratsky got out and opened the door. Nut stepped out.

It was an open space in front of a high building.

"Is this Park Avenue?" Nut asked.

"Park Avenue is everywhere. Where there's money there's Park Avenue."

Nut stood and looked.

"Keep quiet and follow me!"

Nut was silent. He knew that if he talked he might lose his job.

But Nut heard the music in the basement, even at that late hour.

As Nut followed Mr. Ratsky and climbed the stairs, he heard clearly a woman's scream coming from the basement. But he dared not ask anything.

At length they came to an apartment. It was very big and very rich. On the floor there were expensive carpets of the kind one sees in the movies. One room followed the other and then there came a big room with many sofas and small tables along the sides of the walls on which there were many men's and women's pajamas. The light was faint. Nut could see everything, yet nothing clearly.

"Sit down," Mr. Ratsky again commanded.

Nut obeyed the order. He sat on the edge of a chair, trembling.

Mr. Ratsky took off his overcoat and hat and looked at his wristwatch. It was ten minutes to five.

"Take off your hat! Take off your overcoat! Take off your coat. Take off your shirt. Take off your trousers. Take off your underwear! The room is warm, it'll do you no harm. Stay where you are without moving! When the bell, inside, rings, come in! Do as I tell you. Remember! And remember well!"

Mr. Ratsky commanded with a slow, solemn voice. The voice was so slow and solemn that it was full of magic. And because of this magic, Nut did everything he was ordered.

Nut stayed in the room, naked, waiting.

Mr. Ratsky went into an inner room.

In ten minutes, the bell rang.

Nut followed the magical sound of the bell. Step by step he moved forward.

He opened the door.

Nothing was there, just an empty room.

Nut stopped.

The bell rang again.

Nut moved forward again.

The dim light turned to green, then blue.

"Lord save me! Oh Jesus! I am just a Nut! Forgive me!" Nut was screaming.

He saw a tall, slim figure come out of a coffin. A high clown's hat was on his head. His face was red, black and white. His tongue stuck out. He stretched out his arms. He was ready to catch Nut and eat him up.

Nut was screaming and crying and almost fainting.

"Now I feel better!" It was a sound of relief.

Nut knelt down.

"Damn women," a voice said. "They want you to work during the day. They want you to work at night. Divorce, alimony. They're too tricky to be pitied. They're too weak to be tortured. If I were Hitler, it wouldn't be the Jews I'd try to get rid of, but it would be the women. I'd chop the women's heads off and cut off their breasts. I'd make hills of them and then shoot them into the Atlantic Ocean; or use them for pavements and let millions of my Khaki Shirts[9] step on them. Murder! Kill!"

"I'm no woman. I'm Mr. Nut!" said Nut, beggingly.

"Because women are too weak to be tortured, I have to use men, instead. I want to pull off their hair! To taste their blood! Every hair of a man is like a woman's. Every drop of a man's blood is like a woman's. Torture! Kill!"

It was Mr. Ratsky who had spoken. Action followed his words. He began to pull Nut's hair. To kick his body.

Nut screamed and begged.

"You are such a useless fellow. Weak. It's no fun," murmured Mr. Ratsky.

Through pain and anger, Nut hit back suddenly at the stomach of Mr. Ratsky. He gave him one punch after another.

"Now I've met a fighting opponent and I feel better still. Your punches are worth twenty-five bucks all by themselves." Nut heard Mr. Ratsky put the light on. He handed fifty dollars to Mr. Nut. "Rabbit! Here's your pay. Now get out!"

Mr. Ratsky went into an inner room.

Nut dressed.

Mr. Ratsky came out laughing as if nothing had happened.

"Fifty bucks. You can live on that all your life and without worry. To me it's easy money—just like that. I've broken up lots of strikes. I make lots of money!"

Nut picked up the five ten-dollar bills and tore them into bits. He threw them in the face of Mr. Ratsky and left.

XVI:
"I WOULDN'T GET MAD AT YOU"

"Heaven is above,
Hell below.
Nothing in pocket,
Where to go?"

Nut was outside of the building, but the place where he was standing now was not a street. It was the backyard of the building and it had no way out.

While Nut was looking for some way to get to the street, he wondered how it happened that, when he was in Mr. Ratsky's apartment he saw the picture of his ex-friend, Mr. Wiseguy, lying on the table in one of the rooms.

Where was Wiseguy now?

As soon as the fight had started, Mr. Wiseguy and Miss Digger left together.

They walked towards Fifth Avenue.

"How come that you have a fellow like Nut for your friend?" asked Miss Digger.

"Well," replied Mr. Wiseguy, "I have a good heart and 'pity the weak and have mercy on the dumb' is my principle."

Miss Digger applauded with a sarcastic smile and her favorite expression, "Oh yeah!"

"What do you mean by 'oh yeah'? Don't you believe me?" protested Mr. Wiseguy.

"Of course I do. You are as good-hearted as our Lord Jesus Christ!"

"You're such a darling, I can't hide the truth from you," said Mr. Wiseguy.

"My dear Mr. Wiseguy, please tell me the true story."

"It was just a psychological reason. For instance, if there were no Third Avenue, and no Bowery, there would be no Fifth Avenue and no Park Avenue. If there were no J.P. and no J.D.[10] there would be no Bums and no Trash.

"But because there is a Third Avenue and a Bowery, that makes Fifth Avenue and Park Avenue superior. And because there are Bums and Trash, that makes J.P. and J.D. great."

"Mr. Wiseguy, if you don't mind, please answer my question— why was it you had Nut as a friend?" Miss Digger interrupted.

"My dear lady, here you are. It seems to me, you are just a Darling. By the way, you are very beautiful, it seems to me." Mr. Wiseguy used his right hand to caress Digger's face. Miss Digger protested:

"Don't never do-o that, you nasty man.

Like me a little less,

Love me a little more."

"The reason I was a friend of Mr. Nut was that the combination of Nut and myself made me, Wiseguy, become Wiser, and, of course, Mr. Nut became still Nuttier. You see I am a Psychiatrist. I see nothing in this world but Psychiatry."

Again Miss Digger applauded with a cold smile.

"Now I know what you are laughing about," Mr. Wiseguy continued. "You're thinking how I offered only a nickel to Nut, and didn't give him a dollar. My dear lady, even a rich man like J.D. throws away only nickels now, and so, what do you expect of me? The Wall Street papers say that twelve million workers are unemployed.[11] The Communist paper says sixteen million workers are unemployed. I am a Socialist so I take a middle course; I say that fourteen million are unemployed. When I give a nickel to one fellow, that means I am taking the chance of giving fourteen million nickels away."

"The reason why I, Miss Digger, am friendly with Mr. Nut, is . . ."

"Yes, dear? You're my past, present and future! So please tell me," said Mr. Wiseguy.

"Yes, dear, I love you, *Pizzicato.*[12] It is money. Anyone who has money is my friend—Wiseguy. Anyone who hasn't, is not my friend—a Nut," platformed Miss Digger.

When Mr. Wiseguy heard this declaration, he kept quiet for a while.

He put his hand on his pocket to feel if that billfold was still there.

"My dear, don't be afraid! I will not change you for all the rice in China!" said Miss Digger.

"I just couldn't take it, baby! Oh, honey!" replied Mr. Wiseguy.

As they walked along Fourteenth Street, Miss Digger didn't look at the shop windows at all.

Twenty-five cent stockings, seventy-five cent pocketbooks and ninety-nine and a half-cent shoes filled the windows.

As they walked up Fifth Avenue to Forty-second Street, Miss Digger looked at the expensive seven dollars and fifty-cent gloves and twelve dollars and fifty-cent shoes. She looked at the sixty-five dollar new spring model coats and at the mink coats reduced to eight hundred and fifty.

Miss Digger was not only looking, but pointing at all these things with her finger. She even stopped in front of those windows. And she told Mr. Wiseguy about who had given her a pair of shoes and who had promised to give her a sixty-five dollar spring coat. But she thought, Miss Digger told Mr. Wiseguy, that he would be a better friend.

"I wouldn't get mad at you even if you buy me a mink coat!" Miss Digger said smilingly.

When Miss Digger said all this with her mouth, her eyes helped, too.

Mr. Wiseguy took his arm away from Miss Digger.

For it would cost money.

And he told Miss Digger:

"I can't give you anything but love, baby!"

Miss Digger now knew that she should go easy.

They started walking again.

And Miss Digger began to hold Mr. Wiseguy's arm.

They walked together closely.

Mr. Wiseguy smelt something and he said to himself:—"I wish somebody would tell her to get rid of that perspiration odor."

Miss Digger smelt something and she said to herself:—"I wish somebody would tell him to get rid of that perspiration odor."

As they walked Miss Digger was thinking at which speakcasy she was going to make Wiseguy spend his money.

As they walked Mr. Wiseguy was thinking of how he could get something for nothing from Miss Digger and what place he was going to use as a love nest.

Again Miss Digger stopped at a shop window and looked at these things. But she said nothing.

Mr. Wiseguy turned his head away from the window and looked at the sky.

The air was chilling.

No winds blew.

Miss Digger was still looking at the shop window, thinking.

Mr. Wiseguy looked at Miss Digger and again turned his head away from the shop window and looked at the sky.

The air was chilling.

There came April snow![13]

The snow was good for both.

Miss Digger thought, "Now you must stop the open air exhibition and take me somewhere where you'll spend some money. And then . . ."

Mr. Wiseguy thought, "Now you must stop that looking-at-the-shop-window business. And give me something . . ."

A taxi-driver, seeing the situation, stopped nearby saying, "Taxi! It's the last snow of the season. How about a ride to Central Park? It's beautiful out there. Very . . . nice . . ."

While listening to the taxi-driver, Mr. Wiseguy was figuring: "A taxi costs money. But it'll be cheaper than to take her to a speakeasy. And if I know who I'm with, I'll certainly get something for nothing, even in a taxi."

They did ride.

About fifteen or twenty minutes later, the driver felt that the door of his taxi had flown open.

It caused the driver to turn around and he saw that the two customers had disappeared. But in another moment he realized the situation.

He stepped on the brake and the car made a sudden stop.

Because of this sudden stop, the door closed naturally.

Because of this sudden stop, Mr. Wiseguy and Miss Digger both fell from the seat of the taxi to the floor, one atop the other.

It was a long trip. And the bill ran to $3.00. But the driver got no tip—not even a cent.

Oh, yes, Mr. Wiseguy had made him promises; and the driver had hoped and waited. But when Mr. Wiseguy took the lady to the hotel, he beat it. He sneaked out by the back door. And so. . . .

MISS DIGGER BECAME MISS PICKER

"Heaven is above,
Hell below.
Nothing in pocket,
Where to go!"

Nut followed a ray of light and came to the door of a kitchen, which was in the basement of the building in which Mr. Ratsky lived.

While Nut was standing in front of the door and looking in, a fellow asked him, "Where is the Boss?" and then the fellow turned to the door-keeper and remarked: "O.K. It's the Boss's Rabbit. Pass it."

Nut passed through the kitchen and then came to a small and mysteriously decorated night club.

On the stage, the program was going on.

A swivel chair with no back appeared in an open space on the stage. The chair was flat.

A young girl with absolutely nothing on stood near the edge of the chair. An assistant turned the swivel of the chair.

At last the edge of the chair was just high enough to reach the girl's bottom.

Everybody in the audience was standing up and watching breathlessly.

The assistant took out a shiny dime and showed to the audience. Yelled: "Isn't this a dime? A real one? As good as John D's?"[14]

He put it on the chair.

The girl approached nearer and nearer.

Finally the girl picked up that very dime. Without using her hands. Without using her feet. Using but one thing.

The whole crowd was shouting with joy. "We can do what Paris does," people were saying.

Dollar bills and five-dollar bills wrapped around bottle-stoppers flew from all directions. Each was aimed at a particular spot on the dancer and they hit right. The entire audience must have been good baseball players.

At this moment a fellow came on the stage and addressed the audience:

"Since the world war, this country has become the leader of the financial world. Great Britain has been beaten. She is no longer Queen of the Seas. But in the world of amusement, if we can do only what Paris does, then we are only the follower and not the leader: and therefore we shall have nothing to be proud of. I therefore declare that if any girl in this audience can pick up a dollar bill instead of a bit of metal, we will give her a prize. The prize will be all the money we can raise among the audience."

It was Mr. Wiseguy speaking.

Nut wondered how Wiseguy came to be there.

What would happen—Nut thought—if more than one girl could do the same trick? Which girl would get the money?

"What is the difference between metal and paper money?" asked a person in the audience.

"As I am a Wiseguy," answered Mr. Nut's ex-friend, "I know the trick. And it isn't honest. The girl used a magnet. The magnet drew the metal. If a girl did the picking with paper, that would be real skill! I have a plan. An Epic Plan!"

The whole crowd became silent. They thought this was a new discovery.

"For the sake of the honor of our country," Wiseguy continued, "for the purpose of promoting a new sport, I, Mr. Wiseguy, put up the first five-dollar bill. I will roll it up and put it on the edge of this chair. If a girl here can pick it up, she will get this five-dollar bill. And furthermore, she will be authorized to receive the rest of the prize-money. This competition is open to any woman in this room, young, old, fat or skinny. Professionals or amateurs. And this competition will take place once only. There are no obligations. There will be only one chance. First call . . . First call . . ."

All the rich men held out their bills. The bills were all piled up on the floor. And the audience was watching.

These girls looked at each other and marveled how wise this guy was! How could he know their secrets?

There was plenty of money for a prize, but how could they use a magnet to pick up the paper bill?

It was the first time in human history that there was money and nobody to take it.

And why should those sixteen million unemployed kick about having no money?

Silence . . . followed by silence. Silence . . . followed by silence.

Money was piling up, but nobody took it.

The audience was as eager and as excited as if it were expecting the arrival of the Messiah.

Yes. The Messiah was coming.

And coming not from faraway.

Right from the room. Right from the audience!

Here comes Miss Digger!

Mr. Nut wondered how Miss Digger came to be there. And whether she could do it.

Miss Digger stepped on the stage.

Miss Digger took off her clothes.

Miss Digger had absolutely nothing on.

Miss Digger stood near the edge of the chair.

Miss Digger raised her right hand and cried:

"Hello, sucker!

"I, Miss Digger, will now be a Picker!"

The crowd laughed and cheered. And one of the crowd answered and shouted: "It isn't our money we're spending. It's somebody else's blood and sweat. So we are no suckers!"

Mr. Wiseguy turned the chair round a little bit and raised the edge of the chair just high enough to reach Digger's bottom.

While Mr. Wiseguy was turning the chair, Miss Digger stepped back a little bit.

Everything was ready.

The whole crowd was breathless. You could hear a needle drop.

Miss Digger stepped forward inch by inch. The rolled five-dollar bill of Mr. Wiseguy and the body of Miss Digger touched and connected.

The whole crowd was watching breathlessly. Ladies picked up opera-glasses so they could see more clearly.

One! Two! Three! One! Two! Three!

Miss Digger picked up the rolled five-dollar bill!

The whole crowd was shouting! Jumping! And shaking the building!

They approached Miss Digger and shouldered her up.

They circled the floor.

Miss Digger was received like a heroine who had just flown across the Pacific Ocean.

"Give her the Congressional Medal!"[15]

Nut could not stand this craziness any more. He contemplated crossing the dance floor and finding his way out.

As he tried to go out, a spotlight fell on him. Everyone saw him and there were shouts of "Catch the Rabbit! Let's have some fun!"

Many rich men ran after him. Some caught hold of his leg and some struck his back with sticks. Hit and run! It was as funny as the way freshmen at college are manhandled at the beginning of the academic season. Many of these rich men had their Phi Beta Kappa keys!

"Equality for everybody!"

Nut, penniless, had his free show.

XVIII:

A SAINT TAKES A COMMISSION

"Heaven is above,
Hell below.
Nothing in pocket,
Where to go?"

It was half-past five.

Nut went straight to the east side, his old home section.

He walked way down east. He reached Avenue B.

The street was quiet, almost dead. He was ready to turn back to Third Avenue where there were usually more lights and people.

He heard a baby crying and saw a woman peeping from the hallway of an old, dirty, dark building.

The woman waved her hand at him.

Nut thought that at this late hour, something unusual must be happening to make the woman act that way.

Nut responded to her sign. He went towards her.

The woman walked ahead with a little sad smile as the gaslight shone dimly on her pale, quiet face. Nut followed in silence and in wonder.

When she reached the top floor, the woman stopped and pushed an unlocked door open. Both stepped in. The woman closed the door.

She made the kerosene lamp a little brighter. It was a two-room flat. As the bedroom was curtained with some old, worn-out cloth, Nut could not see what was inside. In the room, where they were standing, there were a few things. But nearly all were good for nothing.

There were two electric bulbs. But there was no light.

There was a gas-stove. But it was full of dust.

It was easy to see that the family had had no money for a light and gas deposit.

In front of the gas-stove was a stove made from an old can. On the handmade stove was a pan. In the pan was some water. In the water were some pieces of bread. In the handmade stove were some pieces of chopped up chairs and tables.

On the floor were a few wooden boxes wet with snow. On these boxes were some old newspapers. It looked as if they had been sat on.

In the corner of the room was a large pile of banana skins. Among this heap of banana skins two rats were nibbling.

Beside the handmade benches, on the floor, there was a pair of worn-out baby-shoes. Near the handmade stove was a wet pair of men's shoes. The stove's heat caused these shoes to give off a vapor.

In another corner of the room there was a picture of a young woman with a baby in her arms, a Saint. In front of this picture there were a few candlesticks. In the candlesticks some wax remained. But the candlesticks gave forth no light.

The woman looked at Nut a second without speaking.

She put more of the wood, chopped from chairs and tables, into the stove. She looked at Nut again without speaking.

She put both her hands on the stove to warm them. Again she looked at Nut without speaking.

She went in front of the Saint and crossed herself, murmuring. Then she came back to the stove and looked at Nut without speaking.

She raised the pan from the stove and stirred up the bread and water and replaced the pan on the stove. Then she stirred the fire with the poker.

Her hand trembled nervously and she dropped the poker on a bowl that was on the floor.

The falling of the poker on the bowl made a noise.

And because of the noise, a baby inside of the curtained room awoke, and started crying: "Mamma, me hungry. Mamma, me want bread. Be good, mamma. Me wanna eat, too . . . mamma, bread!"

Another voice, with a whisper, stopped the baby.

The woman moved her lips a little bit. Her eyes looked down on the floor. She wanted to speak. But she couldn't.

There was the picture of a Saint in the corner of the room. And it was her baby and her husband who were inside of the curtained room. No, she could not open her mouth. She gritted her teeth. She held her two hands together in front of her breasts. She clenched them tight. She stepped vigorously on the floor, yet her steps made no sound. No, she could not speak.

Nut, however, was very slow in understanding the situation. But at last he understood. He didn't hear very clearly what the baby had just murmured. But he thought that the woman's baby was sick and that she needed someone to take it to the hospital. So he volunteered and he was very glad to do so.

As Nut talked, the baby cried again: "Mamma, the milkman not come, long time. Mamma, I want milk!"

Again with a whisper, the voice stopped the baby.

Because of many considerations, the woman could not say it.

But because of her own hunger and because of the hunger of her child, and because of the love, kindness, understanding, sympathy and unavailing willingness to work of her husband, she had to say it.

And she said it.

"Can you spend two dollars?"

While she was saying this, her eyes were full of tears.

While she was saying this, she put some newspapers on the wooden boxes wet with snow, to make them softer.

While she was saying this, she took off her worn-out overcoat and put it over the papers and made the bed still better.

Nut though he was, Nut now knew what this woman wanted.

When he saw the tears in the eyes of this woman, heard the baby's crying and felt the silence of a silent night, Nut thought of all that had happened to him since two o'clock Sunday afternoon. Worry. Cold. Hunger. Being beaten. Misery. Wandering. And he thought of the situation he was in now. And of the hope there was for him in the future. And his eyes were wet, also.

He turned his head towards the wall, so that the woman would not see. He felt better. For he was now rich enough to have a quiet place and a few moments of leisure for weeping.

While he was sentimentally overflowing, the woman thought that two dollars was too high. Nut didn't look that prosperous. She thought that a dollar and fifty cents would be all right. She no longer had any moral or sentimental feelings. She had to be practical. She became a businesswoman. She offered Nut a bargain.

Nut didn't know how to respond to her offer. He dried his eyes with his overcoat-sleeve and said nothing.

The woman lowered the price to one dollar.

Nut was still drying his eyes. He didn't turn his head. He still said nothing.

The woman became angry: "Say! Can't you see I'm without any makeup.

"I'm not old. I'm only twenty-three. I've often been told I was good-looking. I'm good-looking now. What?—I'm not worth even a dollar?"

Nut did not say anything. He wanted to leave. But he thought of the snow outside and hesitated.

"Make it snappy; give me seventy-five cents! I'm not a woman of the street. Tonight is the first time I've ever talked this way. You're my first customer. Give me seventy-five cents! And make it snappy."

Nut was wondering how, with nothing in his pocket, he could help her.

The woman became angrier: "I thought that only rich men were misers. You don't look so rich. Be a good fellow. Don't be like Wall Street."

Nut was very sorry he had torn up all those bills in that rich man's apartment. He was angry with himself, too.

The woman became gentler in her tone. She talked like a person pleading for mercy. "Listen, I must have twenty-five cents. Ten cents to buy a basket of rotten bananas, ten cents to buy a basket of solid bread. And five cents to a candle for our Saint. My husband sold his coat two days ago for twenty-five cents. But his overcoat is too old and nobody wants it. He must have an overcoat so he can go out to look for a job. We are hungry. We must have twenty-five cents! The baby is hungry!"

Nut struck his head with his fist. Why the hell did he tear up those bills?

Since she got no answer from Nut, she began weeping again. "Mister, I must have a quarter. A quarter for a good-looking woman. You can't get a bargain like this in the whole world. Be a good fellow. Don't be like Wall Street. Our Saint will bless you."

Now Nut got an idea. He spoke: "Listen. I haven't a cent in my pocket. But I can give you my coat. Tomorrow you can sell it for twenty-five cents the way your husband sold his. But you should use that twenty-five cents to buy bananas and bread and you should not spend a cent for the Saint. Why should she take twenty percent commission on what you make?"

Nut took off his overcoat and coat and put on only his overcoat. The woman was happy. She smiled. For tomorrow she was going to sell that coat and get a week's supply of food.

Nut opened the door and was ready to leave.

The woman was surprised and began pulling Mr. Nut's sleeve. She said, "You forgot something," and drew him to that bed of wooden boxes and paper.

Nut asked what he had forgot. Hadn't he left the coat as he had said he would?

"No, you forgot something!" The woman lay on her bed and began to pull up her skirt. Even in that dim light of the kerosene-lamp, things could be seen.

Nut moved towards the door.

"What? I'm clean!" said the woman.

Nut moved towards the door.

"Say, I'm clean. I'm no streetwoman. I have my husband inside. Can't you see a man's shoes on the floor?"

Nut moved towards the door.

"Say, young fellow, we wouldn't take something for nothing. Our Saint would not allow us to do that."

The husband jumped up from the bed and came in from the other room.

Nut moved towards the door.

"If you take nothing, then we take nothing. We're willing to starve," the wife and husband said together.

Nut moved towards the door.

The husband and wife became mad and put his coat into Nut's hand and pushed him out.

Nut pushed the door open again, threw his coat into the room and swiftly ran down the stairs.

XIX:

HE SUDDENLY LOST HIS
BUREAUCRATIC AIR

"Heaven is above,
Hell below.
Nothing in pocket,
Where to go?"

It was seven in the morning.

Nut walked back to Third Avenue and followed the Elevated
going up town. He reached Fourteenth Street.

He saw Miss Stubborn, with a leather jacket on, come out
of an apartment building. She ran towards Union Square in a
great hurry.

Nut wanted to approach her and express his regrets and
gratitude. For because of an affair of his, Miss Stubborn had
been clubbed. But the street was already full of people and she
was lost in the crowd.

After the fight the night before, in the cafeteria on Fourteenth Street, Comrade Stubborn had wanted to get hold of
Mr. Nut and go with him to the office of the Communist paper
and report the happening, but she could not find him. Therefore she went with other comrades.

When she reached the Editorial Office on Thirteenth
Street,[16] the elevator of the building was not running and she
and the others had to climb up to the eighth floor.

She saw a person sitting on a chair with a pipe in his mouth.
She thought this person was the city-editor and so she told the
story about what had happened in the cafeteria.

He asked her whether this was a Class issue or just a matter
concerning individuals. Stubborn said it was a Class issue, for

Nut was an unemployed worker and he had been only one nickel short.

The city-editor asked again whether Nut was a party member or if he belonged to any other mass organization. Otherwise why should a Communist waste time and energy on him? Stubborn thought that was a funny question. As long as Nut was a worker, it seemed to her, it was enough.

Stubborn and the other comrades demanded an interview with the editor-in-chief.

The editor-in-chief came out from an inner room with a blue pencil stuck behind his right ear. He had a piece of paper in one hand and he was biting the fingernails of the other.

He asked what it was all about.

Stubborn again told her story.

He asked the location of the cafeteria and went back into an inner room. Again he came out looking at a small piece of paper in his hand.

From this small piece of paper he had learned, the editor-in-chief said, that the cafeteria was the same one against which the Food Workers' Union had complained, because it had secured an injunction against picketing. It had been decided to boycott the cafeteria and now there were two charges against the place. The announcement of the boycott would appear in Tuesday's paper, for Monday's paper was already printed.

Comrade Stubborn was satisfied, since it had been decided that the clubbing of Nut's head was a Class issue.

Stubborn and the comrades who had come with her asked the editor-in-chief who the person sitting at that table was— pointing to the man she had approached first. Was he the city editor? Why did he ask such funny questions?

The editor-in-chief smiled and told them that the man was not a city-editor by any means. He was just a college graduate. He was interested in the movement and he was willing to come to this office in order to learn something. He decided that the college-graduate sympathizer had better go to shops and picket-lines to learn things there first.

When the college graduate heard this, he suddenly lost his bureaucratic air and became nervous.

It was not because of her oratory that Stubborn had acquired the confidence of her union, her shop-committee and her Party Unit. It was not her oratory that enabled her to act boldly in a matter like this. For she was not a good speaker.

Nor was it because of her special dancing at the Webster Hall affairs;[17] for she was seldom there and whenever she was there, it was in order to get contributions or to sell some pamphlets.

It was because she was a good Communist.

Occasionally, a millionaire's son or a well-known writer got into a mess at a demonstration and so got his picture in the paper. The publicity he received would be enough; he was satisfied and would never show up again. Stubborn picketed and demonstrated not once or twice—but all the time.

(Some Communists who like excitement do participate in demonstrations. But when it comes to the plodding routine work, they become spiritless.)

Stubborn sold more copies of the party paper than many other comrades. Every time she sold a copy she got the address of the buyer. And she made a note of it and wrote to get that person's opinions. When she found out that he or she was a sympathizer or party member, she thought that her job was done and she passed the address along to a less experienced comrade who could sell the paper to that person from then on. She wanted to use her time on strangers only.

In getting signatures for the election campaign or signatures for petitions of various kinds, she always left the radical district to others and herself approached a more backward and conservative district. Work in a conservative district took more time. It needed more argument. But she thought that it was the only way to make the movement grow.

At the open-air meetings, she always mixed with the crowd and listened to their gossip and comment. And then she reported what she had heard to the speaker! If the talk she heard brought up an issue of general importance, she made a report of her finding to the party—and asked the editor to solve the difficult points in the Open Question column.

When she rode in the subway, she always sat among the poorly-dressed women or men and spread the Party paper out widely so that they could see it; for she remembered how she had become radical. When she finished reading the paper, she always left it on a seat and hoped someone else would pick it up.

Whenever she passed by a newsstand, she would ask the newsdealer for the Party paper. For she knew frequent mention of the paper gave it publicity.

She did these things because she was interested in doing them—not because they were an assignment. Assignments were easily dodged, anyway. She could always have said she had to make a living and she was not a Party-paid functionary. But she enjoyed her work for the movement.

XX:
"YOU! YOU! YOU!"

"Heaven is above,
Hell below.
Nothing in pocket,
Where to go?"

At half past eight Monday morning.

Nut saw many Communists and sympathizers walking on the Northside of Fourteenth Street between Second and Third Avenue. Most of them had placards under their overcoats.

The City Marshal brought a few movers with him and came to the building in which Stubborn's family lived, to bring the family possessions to the street.

The movers complained that the snow had made the stairs wet and that they had to move a sick woman from the top floor down to the street—a trip of five flights of stairs. Perhaps the movers did not care for a sick woman, for she had to die anyhow; but they had to take care of themselves.

And now in front of the building, on the snowy, smudged pavement, there were beds, tables, mattresses, chairs, cooking utensils, papers, clothes and other things; and on all these furnishings snow was still falling.

In the hallway a sick woman lay on a bed, shivering and trembling. Near the sick woman, a middle-aged man stood by. His mouth was open and his eyes alternately looked at his wife and at the things on the pavement.

The passers-by threw pennies and nickels on the mattress and tables.

At nine o'clock a young girl emerged from the crowd and stepped on a table.

It was Stubborn! She spoke to the people there hesitatingly—in broken sentences.

And now placards appeared. . . . The crowd applauded and shouted.

Because of the shouts and applause of the crowd, the girl became more courageous. Her voice became louder and clearer.

"The evicted family is my family!" she said. "Look! There! That man is my father. Look at him again. Look at his face. Look at his eyes. Look at his bowed back. Do you believe that he, my father, is a lazy bum—a man who doesn't want to work?"

"No!" shouted the crowd.

"Look at my hands!" the father cried out. "See how tough and rough they are. I've worked all my life. Only a few months ago, I lost my job."

"Now," exclaimed Stubborn, "look at that sick woman. She is my mother. Do you think I lie when I say she's sick—sick in this snow and cold? The landlord is killing her!"

"The landlord's a bastard!" said a woman passerby.

"Now look at me," continued Stubborn, "I've done everything I could to make a few dollars to buy bread and butter for my unemployed father and my sick mother! Do you think that I should see my father and my sick mother starve and pay the landlord? I have done all I can to make a few dollars to pay the rent. One thing I did not do and won't ever do. . . ."

"Be friendly to your landlord, Mr. System. Everything would be all right! Girl, you've a nice face, don't be so stubborn!" advised a well-dressed fellow.

"How long have we lived in this building?" Stubborn again continued. "A year! How much rent do we owe the landlord? Two months. Are we the only family who are behind in paying the landlord? There are sixteen million workers out of jobs!

"Are you sure that some day you won't be like our family? Maybe it will be you. Maybe you! Maybe all of you! You! You! You!

"Why are you walking in the snow, to get to your work? Why do you live in this poor neighborhood? We are all in the same boat.

"We must all fight against this eviction! When you fight for my family, you are fighting for yourselves!"

"Down with Capitalism!" came a voice from the crowd.

Before Stubborn had a chance to say anything else, some plain-clothesmen, who had pushed their way through the orderly crowd, forced Stubborn off the table.

After Stubborn had been forced down from the table another speaker stood up. The speaker was not on a table nor even on a chair, but on two men's crossed arms.

As the speaker was thickly surrounded by the crowd, the police could not break in.

When the police pushed, the whole crowd moved in the direction of the push—and the speaker went on just the same.

And while the speaker spoke, the crowd moved the furniture into the building, and up into the rooms from which it had been taken.

How long Stubborn's family would remain in the apartment no one could tell. But everyone could see that her family had that day moved in. And that because of the struggle, the eviction had been stopped.

As the fighting went on Mr. Wiseguy and Miss Digger, who had come out of the rich men's night club, passed by and stopped to look on a little while.

Miss Digger had picked up so many five-dollar bills at the club, she felt she was rich, and that she was surely going to move out of that East Side dump in which she had been living.

When the fighting against eviction was going on, Nut was in the crowd. He did all that he could to stop the dispossessing and help move the furniture in again. And he was glad that he had a chance to pay his tribute to Stubborn.

Later when all was over, Nut in his wanderings stopped in front of a ten-cent movie on Third Avenue near Fourteenth Street. A poster made of cardboard, said:

"Prosperity is coming back very soon.
A New Deal!"

Nut stamped his foot on the pavement and exclaimed:
"Damn Liar!"

As he stamped his foot, a dime dropped out from the cuff of
his trousers. It was his dime. It was his long-lost dime! It was
his "prosperity!"

He picked up the dime. He got a ticket for the movie.

He slept there. He slept in a dime hotel.

He slept on a chair bed!

HE WAS SATIRIZING

". . . Try my pill—New Deal!
   Hello,
   Everybody:
   How do you feel?"

When the deal was old,
   We were told:
   "Chicken in every pot!"[18]
   Now the deal is new—
   So the guy is telling you.
   I see no chicken hot.
   And I even lost my little pot.

When the deal was old,
   We were told:
   "There is a little dark spot
   In the sun, you see—
   So the depression
   Hits you and me."

But it's the same sun
   In one country where
   There's no depression—Why?
   And the sun
   Hurts no one!

When the deal was old,
   We were told:

"Prosperity is right around the corner."
Now the deal is new—
So the guy is telling you.
I have bummed around
The corners of the West.
The corners of the East—
Dirt,
Starvation;
But where is prosperity
To be found?

When the deal was old,
    We were told:
    "Don't hurry!
    Prosperity will be back right away."
    Now the deal is new—
    So the guy is telling you.
    I have waited and waited.
    How can I be in no hurry—
    Since hunger knows no holiday?

When the deal was old,
    We were told:
    "Everything takes time!"

But I haven't a nickel,
    Not to say a dime.
    How can I say "Dandy and fine!"
    While in a breadline?

When the deal was old,
    We were told:
    "Hard times are here,
    Because we have no beer."
    Now the deal is new—
    So the guy is telling you.
    We now have beer,[19]
    But is prosperity here?

When the deal was old,
　　We were told:
　　The garbage was full of filth.
　　But we could still have something
　　To pick up, and to chew,
　　In the wind of wintry cold.
　　Now the deal is new—
　　So the guy is telling you.
　　Rotten meat makes chopped meat.
　　When the chopped meat is rotten,
　　It makes sausage.
　　Nothing is left
　　In the garbage!
　　When the winter is over—
　　Here's the blessing of the Deal New:
　　Eating the morning dew!
　　Looking at the mountain view!
　　Or singing the St. Louis Blues.[20]

It's under this system!
　　It's under this system!

Mr. System
　　Beware:
　　The Hanging
　　On
　　Union Square! . . .

ACT III

XXII:

ROARING AND ROARING
AS IT WENT BY

"Try my pill—New Deal!
Hello,
Everybody:
How do you feel?"

It was Mr. Nut satirizing.

While Nut was sleeping, he slept as if he were a dead man. The only difference was that a few drops of water dropped from the corner of his mouth occasionally.

Oh, what a sleep!

But as he had paid only a dime, Nut was not able to sleep without being disturbed.

So Nut became wise. He looked around for a seat in the corner of the house or one at the very end of a row.

While Nut was moving, he passed an old woman. The old woman saw Nut coming and she was trembling and almost crying: "Don't do me anything, Mister," she moaned, "'cause I didn't have a ticket. Don't do me anything, please! Forget it this time! I won't do it again. Be a good man, God bless you." Nut was not a watchdog of the movie house. Nut said nothing.

Nut found a seat at the end of a row.

He sat down.

He was immediately aware that he had sat on a briefcase attached to the hand of a person next to him.

The fellow awoke and grumbled to Nut: "What do you want, anyway? Do you want to steal my stuff?"

"Say, I paid my dime and a seat's coming to me. I am not a

Nut anymore. Y' understand? Your hand and your stuff's got no business here."

"I'm sorry. Awfully sorry. The first principle of a salesman is not to get angry. Say, do you want to buy something? Shaving cream. Only a dime. You need a good shave. It pays to be clean. A shave'll help you make money!"

Nut said nothing.

"I got it—maybe you're a late riser," the fellow whispered in the dark.

> *"Shave in just*
> *Two minutes flat—*
> *Kiss your wife,*
> *Grab your hat."*[1]

"Wife!" Nut answered.

"Well, here you are, then," the fellow again whispered.

> *"You may have your ring,*
> *You may have your flat—*
> *But when she feels your chin,*
> *You won't get that."*

Nut said nothing.

The salesman turned now to a shabbily-dressed woman dozing in a seat and he uttered:

> *"A bearded lady*
> *Used a jar:*
> *And now she is*
> *A movie-star."*

There was no response and he turned to Nut again.

"Say, I can give you a bargain." The fellow pulled Nut's sleeve.

"Don't bother me," Nut said again.

"Say, with the New Deal, prices are going up. My prices are going down. This is your great opportunity, Sir. It happens once in a century. Buy something!"

Nut said nothing.

The fellow pulled Nut's sleeve again.

Nut said nothing.

Nut could not stand this nuisance; Nut had to move.

He saw a fellow walking away from a seat on the other side of the row. Nut passed by the knees of other roomers and again sat down. And again Nut slept.

No, he couldn't sleep now.

Because of all the things that had happened to him last night, clubbing, punching, and beating—Nut was full of pain after he had slept for a while.

So he had to listen to the music. He had to see the show.

The music was something like this:

> "If you want to have your fun,
> You can play with your gun!
> If you want your heart to spring,
> You can pull your string."

Some fellow was crying "Jesus!"

The picture came to a routine climax: a fellow's lips connected with those of a girl.

The sound "Jesus!" arose again.

A person dressed like Mr. Wiseguy—he had no beard, though—began to follow the instructions of the romantic music and started showing some action.

The fellow was so near to Nut, Nut noticed what he did.

Another fellow told him: "I am a medical doctor by profession. You should stop this. It is not hygienic."

Nut began to smell a funny odor.

In the meantime Nut wondered how a medical doctor happened to be in a dime hotel.

Because of the funny smell, Nut moved again.

This time he met the Southern fellow who had taken a penny from him last night.

"You are a liar!" Nut exclaimed. "You said that you would

go to a thirty-five cent hotel. How do you come to be here, then?"

"No, I didn't lie to you. I tried to get a bed. But because of the snow, every hotel was filled up, so I couldn't find any. I have lots of bread with me; take some."

Nut accepted the invitation.

While Nut was eating, he said to the Southern fellow: "I heard some big shot talking about going back to the earth and in that way solve the unemployment problem. And now with this New Deal here, food has gone up, so what in hell did you come to the city for?"

"Those big shots are bluffing," Nut was told. "The rich guys get all the food in the end. We won't get any, that's certain. Say, I owe you a penny. Here it is. Thanks."

Nut hated the money business, so he moved again.

While he was moving, he stepped on the toe of a richly-dressed fellow. The fellow was sour. He was so sour he was yelling: "I'm an ex-millionaire! All my money was wiped out in Wall Street. I'm broke. And goddamn it, I came here. What the hell, you dirty bum, why don't you keep your eyes open? Wheredya get the nerve to step on a millionaire's toe?"

"Some day I'll cut your head off; t'hell with your toe." Nut said this with a little smile.

This smile he hadn't had for a long time.

The seat next to the ex-millionaire was full of vomit. It was wet. It was smelling like a millionaire.

Nut moved back.

As Nut was moving back and looking for his old bed or, if possible, to have some better bed—everybody he saw was, with closed eyes, asleep. He could not understand why the show and the mechanical talking of the screen had to be carried on. Was it not enough just to be sleeping on a seat, while the Third Avenue "L" was roaring and roaring as it went by.

XXIII:

HE FELT THAT . . .

"Try my pill—New Deal!
Hello,
Everybody:
How do you feel?"

It was twelve o'clock.

Nut came out of the movie house.

As Nut had slept for a while, and had got some bread from the Southern fellow, he was not sleepy or hungry any more

Because he was neither sleepy nor hungry and he had nothing to do, the warm sun, shining in the sky, gave him a certain mystical feeling.

As the feeling was mystical, he didn't know what it was.

He felt that he had lost something. But he didn't know what he had lost.

He felt that he had gained something. But he didn't know what he had gained.

He felt that he had been satisfied. But he didn't know how he had been satisfied.

He felt that he had been disappointed. But he didn't know what had disappointed him.

He felt that he was full of joy. But he didn't know what the joy was about.

He felt that he had mental pain. But he didn't know what this mental pain was.

He felt that he had an agreeable, soothing feeling through his whole body. But he didn't know what this agreeable, soothing feeling was.

He tried to forget. But this made him remember more.

He tried to remember. But he didn't know what he should remember.

The feelings he had now didn't come to him when he was very sleepy.
The feelings he had now didn't come to him when he was very hungry.

Because he had just got some sleep and he had just had some bread, these feelings came to him.
Because he had had a little sleep and he had had a little bread, he was a little bit nervous and a little bit sentimental.

Because he was a little bit nervous and a little bit sentimental, these mystical feelings came to him more keenly.
Because he was in a very bad shape, he felt that he needed these feelings more.
He decided that he should do something. But he didn't know what to do.
He decided that he should see somebody. But he didn't know whom to see.
He decided that he should go somewhere. But he didn't know where to go.

His feelings were mysterious.
His thoughts were confused.
His actions were aimless.

Finally, he decided to go to Union Square. For now that the snow had stopped and the sun shone, there must be some persons arguing on the Square. There must be some persons who would tell him where to get a job.
To Union Square Nut walked.

Union Square was west of Third Avenue. Nut didn't know why he crossed Third Avenue and walked to the place where, two and a half hours ago, a fight against eviction had taken place.

He came to the entrance of the building in which Stubborn lived.

He then realized what all these mysterious feelings were about.

He hurried hack.

As he was passing the shopwindow next door he looked at himself reflected in the window-glass.

He laughed.

He laughed so hard that he himself could hear his laughter.

When the laughter was over he began to feel ashamed of himself.

When he crossed Third Avenue and reached the other sidewalk, he saw his shadow on the pavement. He protested. He had his four reasons as to why he should not retreat.

These four reasons Nut first evolved in his brain; then he wrote them down, in outline, on a bit of paper.

The points he made were logical, reasonable and scientific!

Because they were logical, reasonable and scientific, he had courage.

Because he had courage, he went back towards Third Avenue.

Again he reached the building in which Stubborn lived.

He walked through the hallway.

He went from one step of the stairs to another.

He reached the door of Stubborn's apartment.

All those four reasons that he had found, gave Nut the courage to come there.

Suddenly, he discovered that he had no reasons at all.

If he had forgot and left his hat here when he had been helping the family to move the furniture back, he would have had a reason.

If he had promised her a book and now was coming to give it to her, he would have had a reason.

If he had borrowed a nickel from her last night in the cafeteria and now was coming to return it, he would have had a reason.

If he had dropped his pencil in the apartment and now was coming to get it, he would have had a reason.

Nut had none of these excuses. Nut had no reason.

———

Oh yes, Nut had his four reasons!

But could he tell her that he was coming here to show his appreciation of her beauty?

No.

Could he tell her that he was coming here to show his admiration for her bravery?

No.

Could he tell her that he was coming here to show his gratitude for her friendship?

No.

Could he tell her that he was coming here to show his recognition of her comradeship?

No.

He had the guts to hit the police. But not the guts to knock at this door.

He had the nerve to struggle and try to get hold of the pistol of a policeman. But not the nerve to knock at this door.

He had to leave.

And he left.

XXIV:

IT WAS ONLY BECAUSE . . .

"Try my pill—New Deal!
Hello,
Everybody:
How do you feel?"

It was twelve o'clock.

Stubborn was sleeping.
   While she was sleeping, she was thinking.
   One thing was irritating her.
   During the fight against the eviction, she had seen that college-graduate Mr. Would-Be-Bureaucrat standing across the street, academically watching. That was the way he was taking the advice of his editor-in-chief to have some direct experience of the class struggle and to show solidarity with the working class.
   Her feeling was too personal, Stubborn thought. She was finding fault with the college man because he was not helping her family. Yet the matter of Mr. Would-Be-Bureaucrat did not concern her alone. It concerned many, and he had quite a few brothers and sisters.
   Many blah-blahed on the platform and rattled and prattled in the paper's columns. For they knew the best quotations from the radical books and they knew more of grammar and spelling though what they said and wrote was not understood by the workers and sometimes spread poison among them.
   Sometimes, these bureaucrats were exposed and kicked out of their positions. But a month or two later, they would again become prominent. For they not only knew how to get to the top and how to keep on the top. They also knew the technique of getting back to the top.
   Their best card was, they did not defend Bureaucracy. They

themselves pretended they were of the workers. Together with the workers and good leaders, they yelled "Down with Bureaucracy!" And so they got the cheers and the applause of the workers and the confidence of the leaders.

While Stubborn was thinking, she made a decision. From now on she must give some time towards improving herself.

If one does too much self-improvement and no party-work one is not a good communist.

If one does too much routine-work, and doesn't give time to self-improvement, that helps to create a Bureaucracy—one is not a good communist either!

She had decided. The question was settled.

She could sleep now.

But she had some mystical feeling, too.

As the feeling was mystical, she also didn't know what it was.

As she herself could not make out what this was all about, she could not tell her mother.

As her feeling did not bring up an issue of a class nature—in the narrow sense—she could not present the matter at her Unit-Meeting.

If her girl friend had been with her, Stubborn could have talked the matter over with her.

About one hour before she had telephoned her girl friend and asked her to tell her employer at the dress-shop that she—Stubborn—was sick and could not go to work that day. But Stubborn didn't tell her friend about the feeling she had now.

Such a feeling had to be talked about face to face with some-one, and not over the phone.

At the time Stubborn had phoned, she hadn't known she could have such sentiments. They were very recent.

Even at that very moment, she was still uncertain what her feelings were.

"Drop the issue!" Stubborn said to herself. "Sleep! Four o'clock this afternoon, there's a demonstration in front of City Hall. And it's twelve now!"

When she thought of the City Hall demonstration, she began to realize that she had forgot something.

At the time the new Comrade (Nut) was helping her family move the furniture back into the apartment, why didn't she tell him about the demonstration? As he was a new Comrade, wasn't it necessary that he should know about it? If he knew, he would go.

She read the paper and she knew that many communists, while picketing and in demonstrations, had been killed by the police in Detroit and other cities.[2]

She might have been killed last night in front of the cafeteria, or in the activity that morning, or she might be killed in the next demonstration. Who could tell?

Therefore, Stubborn thought, what a revolutionist should keep in mind was to get some new person into the ranks. Then the workers' movement would be like a stream passing under a bridge. There are not always the same drops of water in it, but there is always a stream. So individuals might come in and go, but the movement would go on forever.

If an old member got a new member, Stubborn thought, and that old member were killed, in the Wall Street term, it would be "fifty-fifty." If an old member got two new members and then was killed, in the Wall Street term again, it would be "making money!"

Stubborn knew that she should have told Nut about the City Hall demonstration to be held that afternoon. But she didn't know why she hadn't.

The first few times she had met Mr. Nut she had been very free and very natural. She could say what she felt like saying. She could look at him as freely as she wished.

But that morning, when this new comrade was in her home, she dared not look at him when he was looking at her. Yet she could look at him when he was not looking at her.

While she had been talking on the platform in front of the building, she had been courageous and eloquent.

But when she had met this new comrade, that morning, she had felt that she had much to say, but that she could not say it.

That morning, she had wanted to shake hands with him. She had put out her hand and then drawn it back.

When the Comrade was leaving her apartment, she did so at last. It was only because her mother had said that she should shake hands with the Comrade for his kind-hearted work in moving the furniture.

All this uneasiness of looking, speaking, handshaking and for-getting to tell him about the City Hall demonstration was mystical.

XXV:
WHAT NOW? AND HOW!

"Try my pill—New Deal!
Hello,
Everybody:
How do you feel?"

One o'clock.

Nut reached Union Square.

When he passed the Russian movie-house,[3] he stopped for a minute to look at the posters in front of the theatre. On the poster, he saw Russians who were well-fed and who were smiling.

He had read in the newspapers that starvation had been going on in Russia for years. And he now wondered what these Russians were made of. Iron? Steel? If not of iron or steel, how could they last so long? For it was only about twenty-four hours in which he had gone hungry and he was in a nice fix already.

When the area was clear of traffic, he crossed Fourteenth Street and came to the Square proper.

He passed a statue of a rider on a horse.[4] As he looked up, the fellow stopped him with his right hand:

"Go back to the earth—the nation will have a rebirth!"

"Down with landlords!" Nut replied.

Following the stone wall on the Square, he went towards the northeast.

Nut met another fellow with a sword at his waist. He had one hand stretched out and was shouting:

"Achetez-Vous, joli Monsieur, Ma Belle Demoiselle;
Beaucoup Merci, Bon Nutt, Bonsoir, Bonjour—"[5]

Nut didn't know French, but he guessed that this fellow must be a French salesman of the cheap dress company across the street.

"To hell with salesmen!" Nut said.

He went to the North side of the Square.

Then he saw another fellow. This man had a sincere look on his face. He was standing there, perspiring. He Gettysburged:[6]

"Stay away from the land,
  The factories need cheaper hands!"
"Down with capitalism!" Nut shouted.

Nut followed the stone wall towards the west.

Theoretically, Nut, ever since he had stepped into the Dime Hotel, that ten-cent movie-house, was a Communist.

Organizationally, he wasn't; for things must take time.

At one of the entrances to Union Square Park, he saw a water-fountain. He stopped and had a free drink. Then he took out his toothbrush from an upper pocket of his overcoat and brushed his teeth, without using toothpaste. For he couldn't find any in any of his pockets.

While he was using the water of the fountain to brush his teeth, some fellows, standing in back of him, surprised at what he was doing, laughed at him and sneered at him. Another fellow pushed him away and exclaimed:

"We've nothing to chew on, anyway, so what do we need our teeth for?"

Nut now walked to the center of the Square.

He saw several workmen with overcoats on, very quickly removing the snow that remained on the ground. And he told one of them:

"What are you hurrying for? You hurried before and that's why you became what you are today. Go ahead—hurry today—what'll become of you tomorrow? There's one country where the more you produce, the quicker you get in the bread-line. Take my word for it. I'm not a Nut any more."

Having become class-conscious so suddenly, how did Nut come to know about laws and conditions in Russia?

For to know what you know takes time. To become conscious of what you should be conscious of, takes you a day or an hour or a minute—or even a second.

Nut wanted to know who those three fellows in the Square were. But at this moment, it was more urgent for him to find a washroom than to bother about the historical background of the Three Statues.

When Nut came out of the washroom at the north end of the Square, he saw some people around the flagpost. They were arguing.

It was rather boring, so Nut left.

He saw a group of people following a person with a wheelbarrow in front of him. In this wheelbarrow there were an old, torn broom and a shovel.

There was a sign on his back. It read:

"This is no stunt! I want to show that I am willing to work . . . if I can have a job. As an ex-serviceman, I refuse to starve or stand in the breadline. Work or bust!"

This ex-serviceman crossed Fourth Avenue and pushed his wheelbarrow to the front of a colonial, red-brick building— Tammany Hall.

"You lazy bum, why don't you shovel the snow?" a well-dressed man, who was passing by, told the fellow.

"I registered all right. I got up early this morning and I waited for a long time in front of the office, but I couldn't get the job."

"That's Communist propaganda!" another gent said.

"Last election I voted for Roosevelt. What do you think I am?" the ex-serviceman replied.

While the ex-serviceman went along the Square, no policeman bothered him. In front of Tammany Hall, however, the law had to maintain its dignity.

"Move on!" a cop told the ex-serviceman.

"Where should I move?" answered the ex-serviceman stubbornly.

"I don't care where you move, as long as you get the hell outa here!"

"Say, I'm an ex-serviceman. Stop pushing me!"

"You're too damn fresh. I'll take you to the station."

"O.K., go ahead," the ex-serviceman answered.

"Awright then, come with me!" ordered the policeman.

"If you want me to go with you, push the wheelbarrow for me. I know the law. You can't bluff me."

Another policeman came along. One got hold of the ex-serviceman and the other pushed his wheelbarrow. They all went off.

"Join the Navy, see the world!"
    "Join the Army, have a ball game!"[7]
    What now?
    And how!

XXVI:

WHICH TASTES BETTER?

"Try my pill—New Deal!
Hello,
Everybody:
How do you feel?"

Nut came back to the Square. He was hungry.

An old woman with a basket on her arm was selling twisted pieces of salted cake. "Two pieces for a nickel. Good! Fresh!"—was her cry.

Nut had no nickel.

A few steps away he saw an old fellow who was displaying some clothes on the pavement. Because the pavement was wet, he had put an old carpet between the clothes and the pavement. A few people stood nearby and were looking on.

Nut joined the people who were looking on.

He realized that the old man was a petty businessman of the kind he had seen in the so-called "open market" under Williamsburg Bridge in the lower East Side.

Nut traded his rather good overcoat for an old coat and an old overcoat with the man, and he had twenty-five cents from him as a bargain.

For ten cents he bought four large Jewish pretzels from the old woman on the Square. He found a seat on a park-bench and began to eat.

While he was eating, a fellow next to him looked at him attentively.

The fellow had his thin hair nicely combed. He had a small button with an American flag on it, attached to the collar of his overcoat.

Nut, in the first place, didn't like the guy's face and secondly, he didn't like the way he publicized the Star Spangled Banner. He therefore turned his head away from the fellow and chewed by himself.

But this fellow pulled Nut's sleeve and said to him:

"A fellow was discovered in the Hudson River off Essex Street, Jersey City, with four pennies in his pocket."

"I've got fifteen pennies. I'm all right," answered Nut.

"What! You've fifteen pennies? You must be a rich man!" exclaimed the fellow, surprisedly.

Nut again turned his head away from him. He kept on chewing.

"How do those big-time pretzels taste, good?"

"Why don't you ask the publicity button which you so royally pinned on the collar of your overcoat?" answered Nut.

"You know, the newspapers said that a young chap about twenty-three years of age committed suicide by gas. The chap wrote a note just before he went. The note said that at the very beginning of his suicide his blood was pounding. He wasn't in pain. And he must have gone to another world happily." The fellow disregarded the coldness of Nut and continued his broadcasting.

Nut replied, bored: "I don't believe in another world. I'm going to stay in this world any way I can."

"You know, an artist jumped from the Washington Bridge last night. He left a message. It went something like this: 'If you cannot hear the cry of starving millions, listen to the dead!'"[8]

"No, I didn't know about that artist. I'm no artist myself," said Nut, still bored.

"How is that elephant-pretzel tasting?" the fellow said diplomatically.

"Don't ask me, chap. Why not ask our American Flag? I know what you want, all right!"

"Here's another story: Almost at the moment that the mighty U.S. Navy dirigible Akron was sailing majestically past the Empire State Building three days ago, an unidentified man leaped from New York's loftiest observation tower.[9] He plunged from the landing on the hundred and third floor. But he reached only the eighty-seventh floor."

"Is that the way to be on top of the world?" asked Nut. "I've no ambitions of that sort any more."

Nut had finished three pretzels by this time.

"You have one big pretzel left. Do you think it's as good as the others?"

"At least it'll taste better than a Flag-button."

Nut stopped chewing.

"Do you know how many people killed themselves in 1931? How many in the year 1932?" The fellow kept on chattering.

"If a fellow kills himself, I've no use for him. And I don't care how many poor guys end it all," said Nut.

"Do you want to see a newspaper clipping?

"20,008 committed suicide—1931.
    23,000 committed suicide—1932."

"Don't bother me!" Nut again turned aside from his bench companion.

"Look! See here!" the fellow took out a bit of newsprint from his pocket.

"To hell with newspapers," Nut muttered and he tore up the clipping.

"You'll have to pay me for this," said the other fellow angrily.

"Who asked you to show it to me? Do you want me to commit suicide? So you can take my fifteen cents?"

"You gotta pay me for this paper. Otherwise, I'll call the police. You have violated my property rights!"

"Hell with the police! Go to the Station and get out a warrant for me. You think I care?" Nut now showed his stubbornness.

The fellow saw that Nut could not be frightened, so he began to show his smile. He told Mr. Nut: "If you give me that piece of wonderful pretzel, it'll be square."

"I don't care about that pretzel. I've given away enough money to buy tons of pretzels. But I hate to see a guy like you with your thin hair so nicely combed, think he can take advantage of me. I'm not a Nut any more."

"All right. O.K. Suits me. Fine. Nice. Nice weather. We're friends. If you just give me that pretzel I'll appreciate it very much."

"If you take that flag-button away, I'll give you a nickel and you can buy two pretzels. I can get along without a flag-button, so what do you want one for? I let mine go at ten o'clock this morning, just before I stepped into a cheap movie-house, which was my Dime Hotel." With these words Nut started to eat his last (and just as good as the others) pretzel.

The fellow took Nut's nickel. But he hid the button inside of his coat.

It seems that pretzels tasted better than flags!

XXVII:

"TIME IS MONEY"

"Try my pill—New Deal!
Hello,
Everybody:
How do you feel?"

On one hand Nut was wondering about his own future. On the other hand, he was wondering what had happened to Miss Digger and Mr. Wiseguy last night in the Rich Men's Club.

When Mr. Wiseguy and Miss Digger reached Miss Digger's apartment after the great and celebrated performance in the Rich Men's Club, and had unintentionally viewed the eviction on Fourteenth Street, it was ten o'clock Monday morning.

The first thing they did when they got in the apartment was to have a few cups of black coffee from Miss Digger's kitchenette.

After the black coffee, they opened their purses and divided up the prize-money.

Each had made two hundred and fifty dollars, twelve cents and a half.

Just for a few hours' work!

Rich men had the money. And they were sporty enough to spend it.

The money caused them both to be full of high spirits and gave them both a refreshed feeling.

The two cups of black coffee not only made Wiseguy hungry for doughnuts, but gave him a keen appetite for Miss Digger.

He began to kiss her—to kiss her passionately.

Miss Digger knew what that meant. Here was another attempt at business.

She took off her dress and put on her pajamas. She put some

powder and perfume on her face and body so as to increase the desire of a would-be-customer.

Mr. Wiseguy grew hungry.

"You mean you want to see me?" asked Miss Digger, as her eyeballs shifted to the corner of her eyes. "May I have your order? Nothing is so small as not to interest me. Nothing is too large for me to handle." And she pressed her body closer and harder to Wiseguy.

Wiseguy suddenly became business-conscious and pretended to be dumb. He answered: "Am I not seeing you now?"

Mr. Wiseguy moved his chair back a little. Digger sat on a chair too, for she thought if she showed too much enthusiasm, Wiseguy might ask her to pay him.

While Miss Digger meditated, Wiseguy thought that this girl must be the Digger of Diggers.

When Miss Digger saw Wiseguy contemplating her, she loosened her pajamas in front to advertise her breasts a little more, and lifted the lower part of her pajamas to give her thighs a little more publicity.

Mr. Wiseguy, tempted by her charms, left his chair, and went over to her and began to kiss her again.

"It pays to advertise!" Digger thought, "Publicity means something!"

"Don't be so business-like! I'm your manager," said Wiseguy, beggingly.

"If I can't dig money from my manager, how can I dig it from others? And how are you going to get your commission from me?" Miss Digger asked.

Wiseguy thought! . . .

"It sounds right. But she is too much of a gold-digger anyhow." He hesitated for a while. But he kissed Digger again.

"If you don't give your order now, I'm going to hand you a bill charging you for those kisses," the lady said.

Wiseguy made up his mind and handed her three dollars.

"Just a minute. What do you think I am? Me—a champion of rich men's night clubs? Me—only three dollars? Make it snappy, now. Hand me a five-dollar bill. The higher my prices, the more commission you, as my manager, will get." While Digger was saying this, she made herself ready.

Wiseguy thought of his future commissions, so he didn't bargain.

Digger took his bill and stuck it into her stocking.

On the one hand, Wiseguy was happy, for he was going to get something. On the other hand, he was mad, for Digger was going to take money from her manager!

Miss Digger fixed the window-shade and made sure that it would not spy for Mr. Sumner.

Mr. Wiseguy tried to turn the electric light on.

"It doesn't work, please light the candle!"

Wiseguy lighted the candle.

Miss Digger called:

"Time is money, hurry up."

Wiseguy answered:

"I am going to make you lose money!"

Miss Digger looked at Wiseguy.

Miss Digger looked at the candle.

"What, depression? End of the Roman Empire?" Miss Digger asked surprisedly.

Wiseguy opened a little tin-box and had a few pills of the New Deal.

Miss Digger looked at Wiseguy.

Miss Digger looked at the candle.

Growing,

Growing,

Grown.

"Time is money!" Miss Digger called again.

"I thought you were a liberal!" said Wiseguy reprovingly.

"I made two hundred and fifty dollars, twelve and a half cents just for one night. I'm a conservative now," answered Miss Digger.

"Look at me! I made as much money as you, but I'm still a Socialist."

Miss Digger's breath was short.
  Miss Digger's forehead was perspiring.
  Miss Digger's cheeks were hot.
  Miss Digger's eyes were half-closed and half-open.
  Miss Digger's eyeballs were watering.

Mr. Wisguy kissed her lips.
  Mr. Wiseguy kissed her breasts.
  Mr. Wiseguy kissed her every part.
  Kissing and kissing; but no further.
  Mr. Wiseguy played with her lips.
  Mr. Wiseguy played with her breasts.
  Mr. Wiseguy played with her every part.
  Playing and playing; but no further.

Miss Digger became mad and nervous. She almost cursed.
"This is the first time in my life this has happened. You're
gonna lose your gal!" she angrily exclaimed to Wiseguy.
  Wiseguy smiled sweetly and told her: "That was an introduction. Now is the time."

Miss Digger raised her head.
  Miss Digger looked at Wiseguy.
  Miss Digger looked at the candle.
  It was full of enthusiasm.
  Flaming as Hitler.

Half-past eleven.
  The Right Honorable Mr. Wiseguy and Lady Digger married.

The electric lamp with its wire connected to the reading lamp
on the bed, swayed—first in waltz rhythm, then in a fox-trot,
then in a tango, and finally in the rhythm of the St. Louis
Blues.
  The bird was inspired by the rhythm and noticed that the
snow was over and that spring was coming.
  A bull-dog was lying on the carpet. It watched jealously.

The cat was suspicious. It suspected that another cat had stolen food from its bowl.

Ten minutes and ten seconds past twelve.
The Right Honorable Wiseguy and Lady Digger "Reno'd."[10]

"Time is money!" Miss Digger lost money
"Time is money!" Mr. Wiseguy made money.

XXVIII:
HE LOOKED LIKE A MAN

"Try my pill—New Deal!
Hello,
Everybody:
How do you feel?"

Half past two.

Wiseguy went to the Rich Men's Club to attend the "Conference for Saving Capitalism," after he left Miss Digger's apartment.

He first met Mr. Ratsky.

And then, in walked Mr. System, who looked just like a man.

Mr. Ratsky and Mr. Wiseguy stood up.

"Mr. Wiseguy," said Mr. System, "I heard that you were a Socialist. Now tell me: do I look like the funny pictures of wealthy men people see in your labor paper? I agree some capitalists are bad. But some are good. Sometimes they are bad. Sometimes they are good. Some capitalists are fat. Some are skinny—so, you see how ridiculous are those so-called labor papers. What do you say, Fellow-worker, Comrade—Mr. Wiseguy?"

"Yes, your honor, you heard correctly. It is true that I am a Socialist. But," explained Mr. Wiseguy, "I must impress upon you, Mr. System, the fact that Socialists and Communists are very, very different."

"They are now yelling 'United Front'[11]—and I think you had better be practical and take off that pink coat altogether," said Mr. System.

"Are you telling me? I am no Rank and File, I am a wise-guy," answered Mr. Wiseguy.

The waiter brought in some black coffee for Mr. Wiseguy and some whiskey for Ratsky. The waiter stood ready to take the order of Mr. System.

"Please dismiss the waiter and lock the door!" Mr. System whispered to Mr. Ratsky. "That waiter might be a Russian O.G.P.U."[12]

They were all seated now. They got down to business. And the Conference for Saving Capitalism began.

"Mr. System, thanks for your invitation. What service might I render to you?" Mr. Wiseguy asked. He used his Oxford accent, carefully!

"Cut that out!" Mr. System was annoyed and excited. "I hate that English accent. Great Britain is our enemy!"

"I thought our enemy was Russia," remarked Mr. Wiseguy.

"Russia is an outside enemy. England is an inside enemy. Since the World War, England has lost her international throne in the financial world. But she has refused to accept our lead ership and is playing politics in Europe in order to regain her power. Therefore, we cannot attack Russia right away."

"I think you need some French wine to soothe you," said Mr. Ratsky. "It is right in this room; I can get it for you without disturbing the waiter."

"Don't mention the French to me," exclaimed Mr. System. "I hate them. You know, they have half of the world's gold.[13] They have the strongest army in the world. They can't send their army across the Atlantic to attack us, but they threaten our pal Mussolini.[14] Do you understand me?"

"Just a minute, let me offer you some Japanese *sake*. It's good stuff." Mr. Wiseguy took out a flask from his left hip-pocket.

"I hate the Japs. Damn the Japs. They are sneaky, tricky and goddam double-crossers! They promised when they got to

Manchuria[15] they'd be satisfied and go ahead and attack Russia. That was why we asked our State Department to protest and insist on the Open Door Policy,[16] and at the same time we secretly sold munitions to the Japanese, and also asked the Chinese Nationalists to make concessions. But do you know what those Japs did? Once they got Manchuria they started marching southward. They were afraid of those Russians, that's why. And they are now increasing their navy, they are fortifying the islands in the Pacific Ocean. Some day there'll be some hard fighting in the Far East."

"Since you are so much concerned with the Chinese," said Mr. Wiseguy, "let me offer you some Chinese rice-wine fresh from Chinatown." Mr. Wiseguy put back the first flask and took out another from his right hip-pocket.

"Say! Don't mention the Chinese. I am disgusted with them. I am nervous about them. Those Chinese Nationalists are useless. In outside matters, they cannot beat back the Japs, and within China, the Reds are becoming stronger and stronger. You know, one-fourth of the Chinese population is now under Communist control. One-sixth of the whole Chinese territory has become Red. Those Nationalists are losing ground every day. I really can't tell what things will be like in China in the time to come. Now it is 'China Red'. In times to come, there will be a Red China. What is happening over there is a bad example for India! The Philippines! Bad! Bad!—No, Sir, I don't want any Chinese stuff."

"But you must have something," said Mr. Ratsky plaintively.

"I want nothing but a Havana cigar. Latin America is safe—at least for the time being."

"What do you want from me?" inquired Mr. Wiseguy.

"Work out a plan! An Epic plan!"

"I'll do my best," said Mr. Wiseguy solemnly. He then rose and put on his overcoat.

"Mr. System," whispered Mr. Wiseguy rapidly, "just a minute, now. I want to ask you something in private before we separate. I have two hundred and fifty dollars, twelve and a half cents, and I need two hundred and fifty dollars more in order to buy typewriter paper on which to type my thesis. Unfortunately, my bank is closed. So may I have the privilege of being trusted by you." While Mr. Wiseguy whispered, he held all his commission money of the night before in his hand and showed it to his financial friend, as collateral.

"Beg your pardon! Here is my check," Mr. System wrote something on a piece of paper and handed it to him.

The meeting was adjourned. It was half past three.

In twelve hours Mr. Wiseguy had made five hundred dollars, twelve and a half cents. Who said there was a depression?

Mr. Wiseguy walked along Fifth Avenue. As he walked he whistled with an Epic air.

XXIX:

LUCKY, HOWEVER

"Try my pill—New Deal!
Hello,
Everybody:
How do you feel?"

Stubborn tried to sleep. But she couldn't.

If she had tried hard, she could have slept.

Yes, she did. But when she was about to sleep, the moaning of her sick mother awoke her.

Her mother knew that Stubborn needed rest and she tried not to moan.

But the apologizing refrain of the father disturbed her. The father thought that as he was the head of the family, it was his duty to see that his sick wife and young daughter were sheltered. And now the father had to apologize!

The mother, besides being physically sick, was sick in mind, too. She thought: What right have I to become sick? To become sick in a time of depression? For she felt that the few dollars her daughter made, though not enough to pay the rent for the family of three, was enough to take care of Stubborn herself. Stubborn could have, on what she earned, a small furnished room and probably enough to eat. But now Stubborn spent all her income for the food of the three. And she had been thrown into the street along with her father and mother and how long they could stay in this place no one knew. The thought of all this made the mother sick in mind. And the mother had to murmur.

Stubborn felt somewhat guilty, too. Because she had worn a little button with Lenin's picture[17] on it, her father and mother had not received Home Relief.[18] The woman who had come to the house to investigate had noticed her wearing it. At that time the investigator had not said that the family would not get relief, but she had remarked sarcastically that if this family liked Lenin so much why didn't they go to Russia?

As the three moaned, apologized, complained, Stubborn could not sleep.

Finally Stubborn slept.

She slept from twelve to half past one.

Because she heard her mother's moaning, she awoke.

Stubborn thought that the landlord was coming and that there would be another attempt at an eviction of her family.

No. There was no landlord. There was no City Marshal.

The moaning of her mother was more terrible than the presence of the landlord and the presence of the City Marshal.

The eyes of Stubborn's mother were staring upward. She was silent. Foam was coming out of her mouth. She was shaking. She was trembling. She was unconscious.

At length she murmured faintly:

"The landlord has killed me!"

"Mother, you must be quiet!" Stubborn approached her mother's bedside and tried to comfort her.

Her mother was quiet now. She was so quiet it made Stubborn hysterical. Stubborn felt her mother's wrist. There was no pulse. It was motionless.

Dead.

The eviction, the snow, the cold weather and the excitement had killed her.

Evictions occurred every day. Stubborn's mother was just one victim.

To the landlord and to others, it was just one more woman dead.

To Stubborn, this dead woman was her mother.

Because the dead woman was the mother of Stubborn and Stubborn had only one mother, she wept.

Since tears were the only property she had and she could use them freely, she wept and wept without stopping.

She stopped when her father asked her to stop.

But because of her father's tears, her own tears came again and came faster.

Her father was a man and a man was supposed to be less sentimental, so he told his daughter that weeping was of no use and that she should go out and tell the Block Committee what had happened and see what the Committee would do.

Stubborn went to the Block Committee of the Unemployed Council.

The Block Committee sent a comrade back with her.

When they reached Stubborn's home, the door could not be opened. Stubborn and the comrade knocked and knocked, but there was no answer.

Stubborn used her key.

They entered the house.

"Father! Father!" Stubborn called.

There was no answer.

The Comrade found her father in the kitchen.

"Comrade Stubborn! Comrade Stubborn! I can't tell you. I can't tell you—Your father—your father—blood—the kitchen knife!—Your father—his throat. Oh!—Blood!"

Stubborn stepped into the kitchen. She ran away from the kitchen. She found that her dead mother was a better companion than the companion in the kitchen—even the face of her comrade was paler than the dead woman's, not to say the face of her father lying on the floor with blood coming out of his cut throat.

Stubborn was not excited now.

She thought it was all a story she had been reading.

No.

This was no fiction.
Real!

Stubborn should not have been surprised that her mother and father died, both within the last hour.

She should have been glad that she had gone to the Block Committee. Because Stubborn had left her father, he had not had the chance, before he killed himself, to kill her, too, in order to save her from future suffering.

A note from her father indicated that.

Stubborn was lucky, however.

A MONKEY RAN AWAY
FROM THE ZOO

"Try my pill—New Deal!
Hello,
Everybody:
How do you feel?"

The New Deal didn't help Stubborn's family very much.

It helped Mr. Nut a great deal. For yesterday, at this time—
2:30 in the cafeteria—he was five cents short on a cafeteria
check and was a prisoner in that cafeteria. Now he had two
nickels all by himself and he was a free man.

While walking in the lower East Side to see what chance there
was of a job, Nut saw lots of shabbily-dressed people marching in the street, four in a row. Some of the marchers carried
placards. Nut was attracted by the placards and could read the
slogans on them easily, for there were not so many and they
were wisely distributed.

Some of the placards read:

"Ten Dollars Weekly Cash Relief for Each Unemployed Couple!"
    "Three Dollars for Each Dependent!"
    "Seven Dollars Cash Relief for Single Workers!"
    (Nut asked himself, "Are they going to get it?")
    "Stop Wage Cuts—Make Bankers Pay!"

Nut was deeply impressed by these slogans.

Yet these poorly-dressed marchers impressed him more.

One couple was so skinny that you would have thought the pair had just walked out of the grave. The woman was wheeling a baby-carriage in front of her. The man carried a stick with an empty milk-bottle upside-down on top of it. Attached to the stick was a waving white cloth. The cloth was a hand-made placard and it read: "We Want Milk for Our Baby!" It was not artistic, but Nut knew that their baby needed milk.

Nut could not understand why the marchers were so serious, so different from the people in parades on other occasions. The paraders shouted while marching. They acted very militantly. But their militancy could not hide their sadness. And some of the women-marchers were weeping—No, they only looked as if they were weeping!

When Nut turned from watching the marchers and looked at the bystanders he noticed something different in them, too. The bystanders, the poor and old men and women, seemed eagerly interested in the parade. Nut understood this: he expected such behavior from them. For he knew that the poor and aged were always good-hearted or sentimental. But he could not understand what made the well-dressed young fellows among the watchers appear so grave and concerned. Where were their wisecracks of the past?

He heard someone say: "Did you see the face of that dead woman? The eviction on Fourteenth Street, just this morning, killed her. How could a sick woman stand cold and excitement at the same time? The landlord, Mr. System, is a bastard—if you ask me."

"I saw the dead husband too. His blood was oozing from his neck. God, you should have seen the bed he was on," said another man.

"I'm very sorry for that girl. Her father and mother both died together—both in an hour," sighed yet another of the bystanders.

"I can't understand things. This is a funny country. Starvation right in the midst of plenty," said a fourth person.

Nut heard all that these people said. But he didn't know what they were talking about.

He pushed forward through the closely-packed sidewalk. He pushed and pushed. He pushed and walked. He went the same way as the marchers went and he went faster. He came to the head of the parade.

Right in front of the parade, Nut saw two beds—one by the side of the other. One of the beds was deeply colored with blood.

He could not see who were in the beds. But he could see the leather-jacketed girl, Stubborn, walking behind the beds. Two girls, supporting Stubborn, walked beside her.

Nut thought that Stubborn's sick mother might be on one of the beds. But he wondered who was in the other.

He joined the marchers.

Right behind Stubborn.

He touched Stubborn lightly.

Stubborn looked at him with weeping eyes.

"I am glad to see you here," she said.

As Stubborn talked to him, there was a smile on her face.

No. It was not a smile.

Nor was it weeping.

Maybe it was both.

From the words of the two girls, Nut learned the whole story.

There was nothing Nut could do.

He went with the marchers. He marched with them to City Hall.

It was exactly five o'clock when the whole crowd assembled on City Hall Plaza. Along with the factory workers, white-collar slaves from Wall Street offices participated in the demonstration.

After the speech of the leaders, two girls helped the leather-jacket girl, Stubborn, to the platform.

No, Stubborn could not speak.

But the beds with the two dead people on them and the tearful eyes of the daughter of the two dead, said everything.

On the platform, Stubborn did not speak.

Nor did she weep.

At this moment two other girls wondered where the little Pioneer was. When they started from Fourteenth Street, this Pioneer was with them. Where had he gone?

There he was!

The crowd cheered.

It was the Russian Brat, as Nut had called him when he had tried to sell Nut a Communist Children's Magazine in the Fourteenth Street Cafeteria.

Nut looked at the Russian Brat who, with a Red Flag, was standing on the porch of City Hall.

The City Hall guards and the police tried to get him down. But they could not reach him. Everyone was surprised how this little boy could have passed through the heavy guard and got where he was. It was a mystery.

The flag which the little boy was carrying was not a regular red flag. It was a starred cloth with a kind of red paper pasted on it.

It might have been a comic feature. In comparison with so big a building as the City Hall, the little boy seemed just like a monkey that had run away from the Bronx Zoological Garden. It was very interesting.

Yet because of those two dead bodies the sight was not comic. And on the Flag Mr. Nut placed his hopes.

A new world.

A better day.

XXXI:
HE WAS PHILOSOPHIZING

. . . There is heat in the sun.
   Vertically, at any time,
   Horizontally, in any space,
   Things must be done.

Out of millions and millions of years,
   This universe came;
   After millions and millions of years,
   It will end.
   Yet
   The world is turning and turning.
   And four-legged monkeys and two-legged monkeys are breed-
ing and breeding.
   The world is turning on.
   The monkeys are breeding on.
   On and on.

Tides must rise and tides must go;
   Rivers dry as rivers flow.
   Flowers bloom and flowers must fall—
   Death comes to all.
   Yet
   Life is going on.
   Going on and on.

We have lived days, months and years;
   We have had both joys and tears.
   But the joys of the past are in vain.

And sorrows remain.
Yet
Life is going on,
Going on and on.

We had joys in days *before* tomorrow,
So, there must be joys in days *of* tomorrow.
But tomorrow's joy belongs to tomorrow—
Tomorrow! Tomorrow! Will there be tomorrow?
Yet
Life is going on.
Going on and on.

We had days *before* tomorrow,
There must be days *of* tomorrow.
Since we can remember only the sorrow of the past,
Who knows if our coming joy will last?
Yet
Life is going on,
Going on and on.

If we cannot remember the sorrow of the past,
We shall not make tomorrow's joy last.
If we can make tomorrow's joy last,
How can our memories in days of tomorrow forget our sor-
rows of the past?
Yet
Life is going on.
Going on and on.

We see the flowers of tomorrow.
We hear the birds of tomorrow.
But tomorrow, where will be the flowers of *before* tomor-
row?
Tomorrow, where will be the birds of *before* tomorrow?
Yet
Life is going on.
Going on and on.

Grave-Diggers with high hats on.
  Their Buryers with Overalls on—
  Faster and faster these Grave-Diggers are digging on,
  Deeper and deeper these Grave-Diggers will go down.
  Yet
  They are digging on,
  Digging on and on.

Grave-Diggers with high-hats on,
  There must be Buryers around to help them;
  If these Buryers are your helpers,
  Why should Grave-Diggers let their stomachs be empty?
  If these Buryers are your enemies,
  Why should you dig your grave and not leave your bodies
above ground to feed the vultures?

By leaving your bodies
  To the vultures
  Your left-overs
  Will be
  A worse curse to the Buryers with overalls on.
  Yet
  The high-hat Grave-Diggers are digging on.
  Digging on and on.

It's under this system!
  It's under this system!

Mr. System
  Beware:
  The Hanging
  On
  Union Square! . . .

ACT IV

XXXII:

A MAN WALKED ON
HIS HANDS

"There is heat in the sun.
Vertically, at any time,
Horizontally, in any space,
Things must be done."

It was Mr. Nut philosophizing.

Half past six when the City Hall demonstration was over. Nut
came back to Union Square.

On the Square a fellow approached him.
"How did you like the demonstration?"
"What do you mean—'like the demonstration?' With two
dead persons in front, do you think it was a picnic?"
"You are very revolutionary, I see! I'm sorry—I'm awfully
sorry. Are you a communist? Are you a Party member? What
unit do you belong to, comrade?" The fellow spoke to Nut in
an intimate tone.
Nut looked at him, looked at him carefully.
The fellow wore a pair of old, wornout shoes and a pair of
expensive socks, which could be seen underneath his raised
trousers. And the suspicious eyes of that fellow's freshly-
trimmed head, resting on a policeman's neck, looked at Mr.
Nut attentively.
It was the same fellow who had been in the cafeteria on
Fourteenth Street last night. But when the fight had started,
Nut had seen him talking with the police, and signaling with
his eyes to some other fellows who had the same suspicious
appearance.

While Nut was looking at him, the fellow spoke again: "What do you think of this?—you know, about two or three months ago, someone tried to shoot the President?[1] Talkin' for myself, I'm awfully sorry the guy missed."

Nut still looked at him.

"If you're interested in my face," continued the fellow, "I've got to tell you I haven't shaved yet. In the capitalist system, the razors are fake too. You know we should kill all those capitalist guys." And the fellow smiled at Nut intimately, and he looked at Nut from head to foot.

"If you want to kill somebody," asked Nut, "why don't you go ahead? What do you have to tell me for?"

"You see, I saw you today in the Communist demonstration. I think I can call you my comrade." The fellow lifted his lower lip a little and turned it to the left of his mouth. By this, he meant to show that something must be done and that he was confident he had found a real friend in Nut.

"Look here—what did you tell the police, last night, in the cafeteria?" asked Nut.

"I say—do you think there'll be rain tonight?" The fellow swiftly changed the subject.

Nut kept on looking at him.

"I think," continued the fellow, "you must be very different from those so-called Communists! Parades! Demonstrations! Those guys are just a bunch of cowards. They're all yellow! Russia is no good, either. Why didn't it send a Red army here to crush the Capitalists—dammit—blow up Wall Street and kill all the guys down in Washington? Cowards, that's what they are, Yellow! They're yellow I tell you!"

"Is that what the police told you last night in the cafeteria?"

"Say, don't be so suspicious! If you're a coward and yellow, too, just say so. Don't throw mud at me." The fellow again looked at Nut from head to foot.

"Were you in the demonstration?" inquired Nut.

"Of course! I saw two dead bodies on the beds. I saw a girl stand on the platform. Beg your pardon!—she was just on a table. And I saw a boy on the City Hall porch waving a red flag. I saw you too. You were right after that leather-jacket girl—Heh?"

"Your shoes are rather clean—you must have walked on your hands," Nut observed. He was getting mad.

"Take it easy! I know you're a good Communist, fellow-worker—a good comrade!" The fellow took an even more intimate air with Nut. He patted him on the back.

"I'm not a Party member," said Nut. "But I don't like the way you discredit the Communists. You have a pair of clean shoes, so you haven't any right to kick."

"This is what I tell you—because those Communists are so damn yellow, I don't care to be mixed up with them. I like action. I want to . . ."—the fellow here made a gesture of chopping someone's head off.

"Is there anything else you've got to tell me?" asked Nut.

"Come here!"

"What is it? I can hear you," answered Nut.

"It's a secret!" the fellow whispered.

Nut got closer.

"If you want a weapon, I have it."

"Where is it?" asked Nut.

"Somewhere."

"Will you go with me?"

"That's why I talked to you, you see," the fellow replied with a hearty smile.

"Let's go," Nut whispered.

"You're a good guy. You're some guy." The fellow looked at Nut with a cold and artificial air of intimacy.

"What's that? What's that?" Nut suddenly exclaimed.

Nut had turned over the overcoat collar of the fellow, and a badge was revealed.

The fellow walked away. As he walked, he looked back at Nut and warned him: "If you hang around Union Square and mix up with those dirty Russian Reds, I'll get you some day." And after these words, he looked back at Nut once or twice more.

The plainclothesman finally disappeared from the scene.

But something remained in Nut's mind.

Nut was thinking.

Because the fellow was a plainclothesman, Nut did not join him.

But because of what the fellow told him, Nut got an idea. He would, by himself, kill somebody.

"Zangara! Only fifty-nine capitalists rule us!"[2]

"Murder! Kill! Go!"

XXXIII:
UNTIE THE TIE

"There is heat in the sun.
Vertically at any time,
Horizontally, in any space,
Things must be done."

A Negro, selling newspapers, came towards him, yelling:

"*Daily Worker*!³ The Only English Worker's Daily in America! Three cents a copy!"

Nut took a look at the headlines and asked the Negro: "What do you think of Zangara?"

"Because of him, capitalists tried to frame communists! We do not approve of individual terror! One capitalist is assassinated and another takes his place. We have to change the whole system!" the Negro answered Nut, and then walked on, to attend to his business of selling communist papers.

Nut began to worry about his plan.

"I don't care about my own life," said Nut to himself. "But if I give the capitalists the opportunity to frame communists, well . . . am I the communists' friend or enemy?"

Nut began blaming that leather-jacket girl, Stubborn. If he hadn't met her twice in the communist cafeteria, three months ago, once last night in the cafeteria and another time this morning in the eviction, Nut might not have been in the demonstration and therefore he might not be suspected by others of being a communist. Then he would be free to do whatever he liked. But now . . .

Nut had to give up the idea of assassination.

He was sitting on a park-bench. He took out his remaining pretzel and began biting it.

While biting the pretzel, he felt physically better.

But mentally, because plans were no longer occupying his mind, he felt restless.

Nut was again lovesick!

No.

He was not going to get into more trouble.

He thought how he could get rid of the trouble he already had.

He was trying to untie the tie.

He was trying to "de-hypnotize" the hypnotized.

For love was pain. At least to him. At least to him at this time.

This was the first stage of the situation.

A few moments later, he began to ask himself whether that leather-jacket girl, Stubborn, was worthy of his love.

He had greatly worshipped Stubborn for her heroism. But now he could not understand why it was that at the demonstration at City Hall, she had just stood on the platform and had not spoken—though she had not wept.

Had not her mother and father both been killed by the capitalist, Mr. System? Then why didn't she take advantage of the occasion and call upon the workers to revenge them?

Would it help any to stand tragically and poetically on a platform?

Nut was disappointed in Stubborn. He had found that Stubborn was not stubborn at all and was just "so-so." She was just one of those girls.

This was the second stage of the situation.

A few moments later he began to worry about the meaning of love.

If Stubborn had spoken at City Hall and had been heroic through and through, would it have been necessary for him to love her?

"Love is a nuisance," he thought.

Hadn't he once loved a certain girl and hadn't he, in the process of feeling mysteriously, thought that if the girl would not love him, he would kill himself? And hadn't he—because he met another girl later, gradually forgot about the first girl—and still kept on living?

"God is love," he had often heard.

"Love is God," he now believed.

"God and Love are the same nuisance and both are the inventions of the ruling class!" he concluded.

This was the third stage of his inward situation.

"Baloney, Nut, you don't really think that," he argued—with himself—a few moments later. "Love is something Nature has given us in order that the species may not be destroyed—that it may exist forever."

"God is no sense at all; Love has some sense!" Nut re-defined.

This was the fourth stage in the situation.

A few moments later he got mad with himself. He felt that the hesitation and lukewarmness of that leather-jacket girl, Stubborn, toward him, were evidences that she was not the least in love with him. And this one-sided, make-believe on his part was stupid. "There is more than one fish in a brook!" Nut reminded himself. This was the fifth stage in the situation.

While thinking, he looked at the other girls who were passing by on the Square. (Fishing?)

He could not appreciate them.

He felt that the leather-jacket girl, Stubborn, was still the only one.

And now he began to think that maybe Stubborn had been too bashful to say what she wanted to say.

He decided that he would ask her about this when he met her next time.

But he did not know where to find her.

And the question he wanted to ask her would be hard to ask even when he did see her again.

So he was rather miserable.

This was the sixth stage in the situation.

Then all the stages got mixed up.

Even as scientific a person as Nut couldn't be scientific any longer.

"Stop your self-hypnotism," Nut warned himself.

"Untie the tie!" Nut advised himself.

"De-hypnotizing" got him more hypnotized.

Untying tied the tie tighter.

XXXIV:
IT AND SHE

"There is heat in the sun.
Vertically, at any time,
Horizontally, in any space,
Things must be done."

The reason that Stubborn had not spoken at the City Hall demonstration was not a psychological one. It was physical.

She had fainted.

She was carried to the City Hospital and she could not even see the bodies of her parents buried.

"This girl is a Red," complained the Lady-Superintendent. "If she doesn't like this country, why doesn't she go to Russia? Now the city has to take care of her and it costs money."

"It will not cost her money, the old hag!" whispered one young nurse to another.

While Stubborn, semi-conscious, was lying on the hospital bed, her problems ran through her mind.

The landlord had killed her mother.

But her father was a suicide.

The father of a communist—a suicide!

She had not been able to convert her own father to Communism; how was she going to convert others?

Yet she thought she had convinced someone who was outside her family.

Even in her present very sad mood she could still remember that Nut had been at the demonstration.

In the midst of all these tragic and sorrowful events she felt, nevertheless, that there was at least one person who had been added to the communist ranks. And he would avenge her family in a definite way and work for the working class movement as a whole.

The demonstration had given many, many workers a chance to have their eyes opened.

And Nut was one of these workers!

Although Nut was only one of them, Nut was one.

A mighty river can grow from one drop of water and a mountainous building be started with one brick.

Because of the significance of the Whole, she had to give attention to this very One.

She had to be glad that Nut was in the demonstration.

Since Nut was only one of many, why was she bothered—even at this moment—when she thought about him?

She now recognized such an unreasonable feeling as Love.

Was there to be love in this world?

No. Since this world, she thought, was filled with hate as a whole, how was it that she, one atom of the whole, had the feeling opposite to hate for another atom?

Was there to be love in this world?

Yes. If love were banished altogether, when the new world arrived, where would the future love find its seed? And why should one worker die now for another, and what are revolutions made for?

As a revolutionist, and as a communist, Stubborn was of the opinion that there was love for the biological reason, for the artistic reason and for the political (revolutionary) reason.

As she was now in such a sad and tragic state, Stubborn had no mind to analyze clearly the reasons why she loved Nut. But she was sure of the fact that among all the reasons there was not, in the least, any buying and selling business.

Stubborn went back to when she had met Nut that morning, and found the cause of her uneasiness.

It was because of the tradition that made a woman "It" and not "She." As an "It," a girl had to be passive.

As a revolutionist and as a communist, Stubborn felt she must overthrow this tradition and stand up and become "She."

Being able to stand up and become "She" was a joy, a privilege and a human right.

To love whom she wanted to love and to express her love— express it openly—that was a revolution.

And to express what she did not love, and to express it openly, was also a revolution.

Stubborn decided that when she saw Nut the next time, she was going to tell him she loved him.

No.
    She was not going to tell him.

Why–
    Strategy?
    No.
Since it was not a business transaction, strategy was not necessary.

No.
    She was not going to tell him.

Why—
    Time? (They had known each other only a short while.)
    No.
Love was just a kind of experiment and time mattered very little.

No.
    She was not going to tell him.

Because if the capitalists knew about it, they would say: "The communists use women to make men become Reds!"

————

Yes.

  She was going to tell him.

For when Stubborn thought the matter over, she felt that if a girl was not governed by the ideas of a cheap movie and was not dreaming of marrying the boss for money, she was not so bad. Let the capitalists say whatever they liked right now. The workers would argue with them, after the revolution, if they could still be found.

XXXV:
"MASSES ARE ASSES!"

"There is heat in the sun.
Vertically, at any time,
Horizontally, in any space,
Things must be done."

Nut slowly and aimlessly circled the Square many times.

The night was getting on: it was growing deeper and quieter.

And the people on the Square were becoming fewer and fewer.

And because the night was silent now, he could hear clearly the talk of the few persons who remained on the Square.

Nut heard talk about the Masses. He heard many words, many phrases. Out of it all, his mind made this:

"Masses! Masses! New Masses; Old Masses!

"Nothing can be said that is new. Nothing can be said that is old. Masses are Asses in all ages.

"Stupid! Selfish! Contented! Short-sighted!

"One burden is taken away; another is put in its place.

"They are always expecting to be saved. But they can never be saved.

"There must be something on their backs.

"If there is nothing on their backs, there must be something around their necks.

"Those fakers know what the Masses are—the Asses. The fakers use beautiful phrases with which to crown them—'average man'—'forgotten man'—names used to get something from the Masses.

"The Communists know too, very well what the Masses really are; and yet they have to say everything good in their defense.

"Make the story short—there is no need to go back to long ago.

"Make the story short—there is no need to say anything about others.

"Just take myself—Nut—as an example.

"As a worker did I join the union? No. For I thought the union was a violation of my individual freedom.

"As a worker did I vote the Communist ticket in the last election? No. For I thought then that Communists were all Russians.

"As a worker did I read and support a worker's daily? No. Every day I spent money to buy capitalist papers and, by giving myself poison, help those papers' circulation and help the owners become Czars!

"If the workers had small cars or radios in their homes, then everything was O.K., and the world could go to hell!

"Mean. Cheap.

"Now these Asses cannot even have the little things they once had.

"With so many workers out of work, how many votes did the Communists get in the last elections?

"In one word, Masses are Asses!

"And I, Nut, as one of them, know it."

As Nut went around the Square, he was nervous, lonesome and miserable. He had lost all the enthusiasm, courage and hope he had possessed while at the City Hall demonstration.

He was so nervous, lonesome and miserable that he slapped his face several times with his own hand. The Square was then so quiet and the slaps he gave himself were so vigorous, that the sound of every one of his strokes was sharply echoed back from the walls of the surrounding buildings.

Nut was not slapping at Nut himself. He was slapping at the Ass. He was slapping at the *Asses!*

Slapping at one. Slapping at many!

Since, during the last thirty-four hours, his face had been hit so often it did not feel pain any more.

So he stopped slapping and instead he started pulling his hair.

He could not see the blood coming out from his head, but he saw the red dew at the root of every hair pulled out.

Now he was full of pain.

Yet he was happy!

And was laughing.

"You Ass! You Asses! You Nuts!" Nut murmured, "This is a punishment for your stupidity. This is your punishment for not being class-conscious!"

Nut noticed the Flagpost in the center of the Square.

Silent.

Still.

Two ropes came down from the very top of the Flagpost to the ground.

At the bottom of the Flagpost was a brass tablet with the Declaration of Independence inscribed on it.[4]

A brisk wind rattled the ropes of the Flagpost and the ropes called: "Come to me, you Nut! You would be a better Flag to hang up on me. You would be the Flag of Starvation Amid Plenty! You would be the Flag of So-Called Civilization."

Nut answered the call.

He crossed the iron wire-fence.

He held one rope in his hand.

He pulled the rope and made a test of it.

He made a knot.

He made a noose.

He took off his hat, put the noose over his head and measured the size of it.

He took the noose off his neck and examined it to see whether it would work properly.

He walked away from the Flagpost, for he had to find something to stand on. And something he could kick away and so have a free swing.

He picked up some stones from off the Square. He basketed the stones in his overcoat.

With the stones he re-crossed the iron fence.

He piled up the stones and made a stand.

He made the noose of the rope higher.

He tested the noose again.

Everything was ready.

No. Not quite ready.

He had read in the newspaper that when a person was alive he might be penniless, but that after his death, he would have twenty-five dollars, for a hospital would pay that much for the anatomical use of his body.

How should he dispose of the twenty-five dollars?

He took out a pencil. He wrote on a piece of paper and willed that seventeen dollars of the twenty-five be given to his land-lady as payment for the back rent of the furnished room he had had. And eight dollars he left as a contribution to the Communist paper to be used for revenging his death.

Nut put the rope around his neck and kicked away the stones from under his feet.

He was worriless—free from care; and rested.

It was twelve o'clock, Monday night.

Mr. Nut ended the story literarily, non-propagandizingly and publishably.

XXXVI:
"WHAT AN INSPIRATION!"

"There is heat in the sun.
Vertically, at any time,
Horizontally, in any space,
Things must be done."

"I've got a plan! I've got a plan! I have accomplished my thesis! What an inspiration!–Oh, what an inspiration!"

Wiseguy threw his hat to the sky and beat at the table with
his stick. He jumped and he shouted.

"It is thirty-five minutes past twelve, young man," remarked
Mr. System, "so take it easy. What did you drink?"

Just then a waiter came in.

"The taxi-driver outside, Mr. Wiseguy," observed the waiter,
"says there is something wrong with the dollar bill you gave
him."

"You see," said Mr. System, "Mr. Wiseguy's dollar bill was
a New Deal, and yet Wiseguy yells, 'I have the solution!'" Mr.
System handed a dollar bill to the waiter.

The waiter left.

The waiter had received one or two bad bills before, himself, but because they had been given as tips he hadn't asked
for others in their place.

The waiter came in again.

"Bring me black coffee! Black! Black! Very black!" shouted
Mr. Wiseguy. While Mr. Wiseguy gave his order, he laughed
heartily.

"The fellow you just brought by taxi from Union Square,"
the waiter remarked, "is smashing everything in the place and
shouting 'Revolution!'"

Wiseguy took two sheets of paper and typed so fast you'd

think he was in a typewriting contest. Wiseguy finished typing his two sheets of paper.

Then Mr. Wiseguy went out of the big room. In about ten minutes he was back. He announced that the sheets had been signed and that every necessary procedure had been gone through.

"The sheets were signed by whom?" asked Mr. Ratsky.

"Tell you later!" answered Wiseguy, mysteriously.

"Lock the door! Let us have the conference," Mr. System ordered.

"To hell with the conference," said Mr. Ratsky grouchily, "if you want some fellows to use fists or pistols or machine guns, I'm ready for you—always. As for me, Ratsky isn't fooling around. No monkey-business for him. I'm telling you, I'm sick of these conferences. They're no damn good."

Mr. Wiseguy disregarded Mr. Ratsky. He asked:

"Do you know how many people committed suicide these last two years, Mr. System?"

"I read in a tabloid," broke in Mr. Ratsky, "it was 20,088 in 1931 and 23,000 in 1932."

"Do you know," proceeded Mr. Wiseguy, "what I heard this afternoon at the Communist demonstration before the City Hall? Some rich Wall Street chaps told me they were disappointed that there were no fresh killings. Two dead bodies, they said, were not exciting enough."

"I know all about that," said Mr. Ratsky.

"I could tell you what those Wall Street chaps might say without going to City Hall," remarked Mr. System.

"Do you know," Mr. Wiseguy went on, "how many persons are willing to pay big money to go to Sing Sing Prison⁵ and see an execution?"

"I am one of those persons," said Mr. System.

"And do you know that now football games and prizefights are losing their appeal?" queried Mr. Wiseguy.

"I'm tired of football and prizefights myself," observed Mr. System. "They're the old stuff again and again. Who wants to see them any more?"

"It's just because they're fed up on things like football that fellows like to read gangster and murder stories," said Mr. Ratsky.

"Well, do you know that unemployment is the worst problem in America and that it can never be solved?" Mr. Wiseguy asked.

"If you ask whether unemployment can be solved, you are a damn fool," asserted Mr. System. "We have to make a noise on the radio and in the newspapers, but we know very well we can't do anything about it."

"Now—you know what I'm driving at, don't you?" announced Mr. Wiseguy.

And Wiseguy took out a cigarette and smoked it with the air of a Messiah.

Mr. System and Mr. Ratsky were wondering what strange ideas were in Wiseguy's mind.

Then the radio was heard:

"A New Deal. Prosperity is coming back right away," the radio was broadcasting.

"This is a funny world," remarked Mr. System. "Nowadays a poet writes as if he were doing bookkeeping. He writes like a business man. And a practical business man talks so naively, you'd think he was reciting lyric poetry he had written himself."

"Well, let's get to my plan," said Wiseguy.

"What is your plan?" Mr. System and Mr. Ratsky asked impatiently.

"Well, here it is," affirmed Wiseguy. "We're going to have some poor fellow hang on Union Square and get Society to come to see him. That is a game. The rich man will get some pleasure and the poor man will get a few cents. The general situation will be bettered accordingly.

"You see," proceeded Mr. Wiseguy, "according to the law of supply and demand, the more unemployed workers there are, the more persons will voluntarily hang themselves. And the more people that hang themselves, the fewer unemployed there will be. As there come to be fewer and fewer persons willing to hang themselves (because of the decrease in the number of the unemployed) the higher the price of a ticket to see a hanging will become.

"It all comes to this: we shall make money," Wiseguy concluded, "and the country will regain prosperity."

"A grand idea! A great thesis! An Epic plan!" exclaimed Mr. System with great enthusiasm. "You are the Brain Trust[6] of all the Brain Trusts! Get started with your plan right away, young man—before the Park Avenue crowd and the rest of Society go to Florida and Europe."

"A good idea! You ought to work it out right away!" Mr. Ratsky agreed.

"What an inspiration!"

Oh!

XXXVII:

SIZE AND DIRECTION

"There is heat in the sun.
Vertically, at any time,
Horizontally, in any space.
Things must be done."

Fake bills hadn't hurt the taxi-driver who had taken Wiseguy
and the fellow with him from Union Square. But they had hurt
Miss Digger, had hurt Miss Digger gravely.

Among the two hundred and fifty dollars, twelve and one-
half cents, only thirty-eight dollars and twelve and one-half
cents were good, sound money.

In addition to these fake bills, Mr. Wiseguy had left with
her a special souvenir.

For, on Tuesday morning following, Miss Digger discovered
that something was wrong with that very property by which
she had made her living during the last two years.

Because of the counterfeit bills and the accident, Miss Digger had to save some money for the coming two weeks. And as
she did not have enough money to see a private doctor, she
went to a City hospital.

Because of the story about Stubborn in the newspapers,
Miss Digger knew that she was in this hospital and she felt
that she should pay her a visit despite the fact that Stubborn
was a Communist.

As soon as Miss Digger saw Stubborn in the ward of the
hospital, she said heartily:

"The things that have happened to you are tragic and I am
sorry for you. The character you showed in the fight at the
Fourteenth Street cafeteria, and during the eviction in front of
your home, is just like that of a heroine in some Greek tragedy.
You were heroic and I respect you for it."

"I'm glad you are with us, very glad," said Stubborn eagerly. "But the fate of my family is just one instance of what happens to a million families. I am just a worker, I am just an ordinary girl and just one of the rank and file of our Party. I am no heroine. No one's a hero, I think. We're just workers!"

"Because of your modesty, Stubborn, I like you much better," said Miss Digger earnestly.

"Today and here, as workers, we are so low, how can we 'modest' ourselves? Tomorrow, as workers, we shall be so high, to what shall we be able to elevate ourselves?"

"I must make clear," observed Miss Digger, "that my private life has nothing to do with those who may hold the same political opinion as I do. I don't want you to look down upon my fellow Liberals just because of me; and I don't want my example to bring disgrace on Liberals in general."

"I know nothing of your private life," answered Stubborn. "I don't believe in what is called disgrace and what isn't called disgrace. Politically we should form a United Front, for the benefit of both our classes!"

Miss Digger looked at Stubborn in a manner that was extraordinarily intimate. Then Miss Digger ran her fingers through Miss Stubborn's hair and then she soothed her face, and then the head of Miss Digger drew nearer and nearer to the head of Stubborn and she kissed her cheek and then her lips.

Miss Stubborn didn't like all this.

"That wasn't so good. I didn't like it," explained Stubborn. "But my dislike is just a matter of personal taste. It has nothing to do with our political opinions. We should form a United Front always!"

"The only ambition I have now," remarked Miss Digger, "is to go to the Orient and do some research work there. The field there for this sort of work hasn't been touched yet."

"What kind of research work?" inquired Stubborn.

"I want to do some research work as a famous Missionary

and woman-author[7] did. In her book, many of her descriptions and some of her occasional remarks about what she has already described were of the same stuff as the pleasure I have given to my customers for the last two years. However, I visited a doctor every two weeks and never peddled disease. But that woman! That woman!" sighed Miss Digger, puritanically.

"Who is that woman?" inquired Stubborn.

"You know—the woman who made money from her Oriental novels! Here is another one of her hypocrisies: She talks about 'Earth' and 'Soil' a lot, but I think what her publishers gave her as royalties was the same thing that I have received from my customers—dollars."

"I told you, Miss Digger, I know nothing about what you've done in the past, but I'd like to know what kind of disease that woman spread?" said Stubborn.

"Outside of what I gave to my customers, that woman gave her readers the stuff that fooled them into thinking that one should become a slave or a concubine. For instance, she would advise a girl like you to be the faithful slave of that bastard, Mr. System. And not only a slave to him when he was alive, but even after his death. Just imagine. The worst part is, that this woman gave advice like this, in the name of Missionary work."

"I, as a Communist, agree with all what you have said except the latter part of your statement. That is what Missionary work, here and abroad, actually stands for! You are still too naive!" said Stubborn.

"And she has been praised by the critics," continued Miss Digger, "as a literary genius. She made every character talk as the writer, an American woman Missionary, was accustomed to talk."

"Congratulations! You have become a literary critic, and you are a sound one! To me how this woman wrote is a small matter!" remarked Stubborn.

"What irritated me most was her repetition and repetition. It made me sick," Miss Digger asserted.

"I guess she had to write more pages. More pages—more money," said Stubborn.

"I must save some money," resumed Miss Digger, "and find something new to do. Look! Whether that very thing of the women there, is formed in the same direction as that of the women here; and whether the shape and size of that very thing of the men there, is the same as that of the men here—this great matter is the only curious subject which our lady-author hasn't as yet touched. She may not know the situation as to the women there, but she must have been very familiar with the situation as to the men there—since she was so sympathetic towards that general, Mr. Tiger.[8] If I can discover the true state of this matter, I would create a sensation and the discovery would be a money-making proposition; to me, of course."

Just at this moment a nurse passed by. This nurse had worked in the International Department of this hospital. Hearing Digger's remarks, she burst into laughter. The nature of this laughter to Miss Digger, meant the solving of a puzzle and the nature of this laughter, at the same time, meant that Miss Digger lost her money-making opportunity.

However, this is a realistic world. Besides her fountain pen and typewriter, Miss Digger had her camera ready.

XXXVIII:
"STRIKE ME PINK!"

"There is heat in the sun.
Vertically, at any time,
Horizontally, in any space,
Things must be done!"

Nut had hanged himself on Union Square.

But he didn't succeed in killing himself.

A few minutes after Nut had hanged himself, Mr. Wiseguy came to the scene, seeking inspiration for his great thesis on "How to Save Capitalism." And he took Nut down from the rope and called a taxi to bring him to the Rich Men's Club in order to hang him profitably at a later time.

Now, Mr. Nut awoke from unconsciousness. But he could not understand how he came to be here in the Rich Men's Club.

Was he in heaven?

And how did it happen that Mr. Wiseguy was with him?

Were all the angels in Heaven—Wiseguys?

Mr. Nut was no longer classic, or particular—a person who stuck to his principles—at any cost.

He would take whatever he could get. He would promise the people here whatever was asked of him and then he would double-cross them.

He had learned at least that much from his life in the previous world.

He was not only thinking of doing some double-crossing.

He would actually double cross, if he got the chance.

At this moment, Mr. Wiseguy, with two sheets of paper in his hand, approached Mr. Nut.

"Sign these two typewritten sheets," Mr. Wiseguy said. "I

saved your life on Union Square when you hanged yourself there and brought you here. Therefore your life belongs to me. You keep one of these sheets and I'll keep one. We are going on a fifty-fifty basis. You'll make money and I'll make money. When you hang yourself, you will leave fifty percent to me. After all, you see, I'm your manager."

Now, Mr. Nut realized just what had happened to him.

Nut signed the sheets—without even looking at them. "To hell with the capitalistic contract," he thought.

"You're a real friend of mine," said Wiseguy, and he put away his sheet in his billfold.

"I'm hungry. Give me food! I'm sleepy, go away and let me sleep!" Nut slapped the face of Mr. Wiseguy.

"The slapping shows his artistic temperament," Wiseguy thought, when he was slapped. "I, as a manager, have to take it! These slaps mean money. Strike me pink!"

Nut was acting nuttily. His eyes, however, were expressing deep thoughtfulness. He was acting nuttily as a soldier off for war. But he was thoughtful as a soldier when he turns his gun.

After eating, Nut went to sleep.

It was two o'clock Tuesday morning.

Wiseguy had to sleep too.

Mr. Ratsky and Mr. System slept also.

While they were sleeping, the four of them were breathing to the same rhythm of "Money—Money—Money"—negatively or affirmatively.

At one o'clock Tuesday afternoon—at the same time that Miss Digger was visiting Miss Stubborn—Mr. System, Mr. Wiseguy and Mr. Ratsky again had a conference.

"It is rather inhuman, isn't it, to hang a fellow just to make money?" said Mr. System, reconsidering.

"You are a capitalist," replied Mr. Wiseguy, "so why should you talk about the word 'human'? Hasn't that word been dropped from your vocabulary a long, long time ago?" While he spoke, Wiseguy held the typewritten contract in his hand.

"I am not at all bothered by the word 'human,' my dear sir," said Mr. System. "But we have to be reasonable. We cannot afford to be antagonistic to the general public."

"Don't try to bluff me," responded Mr. Wiseguy. "In the last World War, ten million men were killed and twice that number of them were crippled and became useless.[9] And what did the so-called public say about this? And how many workers get killed every year because of the speed system[10]—and does the public get sentimental about that?" Mr. Wiseguy now combed his beard.

"Well," inquired Mr. Ratsky, "why don't we start another war? A war would eat up all the goods we have left and would finish up all the unemployed workers. And what an exciting game a war would be! Airplanes in the sky! Poison gas in the air. Hooray!"

"Sooner or later," contributed Mr. System.

"Let's get down to business," remarked Mr. Wiseguy. "I don't think the hanging alone would be so interesting. We have to do something besides." And Wiseguy considered and considered.

"Well, what's on your mind?" questioned Mr. System. "Have you discovered anything? Tell us about it and tell us quickly. Time is money!" Mr. System started looking at his watch.

"As a matter of statistics for the record, it will take fifteen minutes and twenty seconds to have a normal person properly and completely hanged. But during these fifteen minutes and twenty seconds, we could do lots of things. You know, we Americans like jazz. So the first few minutes, Mr. Nut could have his hands and feet—his whole body—swaying to the rhythm of a waltz. In the beginning, Mr. Nut would go slow—taking things easy. Then a fox-trot would be played—and Mr. Nut would go a little quicker. For his breathing will be shorter and he'll naturally go quicker.—Then a tango will be played and you understand, when Mr. Nut begins to feel pain he will have to go faster and faster. And finally when there is no more breathing, and the oxygen in his system is exhausted, he will be at ease and take life just as it is. Naturally, at this time, the 'St. Louis Blues' should be the tune. The members of Society present on Union Square will right after this sing 'Home, Sweet Home.'—What an entertaining program!—Indeed, an unparalleled amusement!"

Mr. Wiseguy here took out his cigarette case and had a cigarette.

"You have shown me the typewritten contract," remarked Mr. System, "but I cannot understand why just because we use Mr. Nut, we have to let him share the profits."

"You said it, that is what I want to know, too," Mr. Ratsky chimed in.

"Maybe," Wiseguy replied. On his face was an easy and sarcastic smile.

"Say things straight out, you," exclaimed Mr. Ratsky angrily. "One more of your wise-cracks and I'll flatten your nose."

"You fellows keep quiet, for my sake," said Mr. System pacifically.

"Why should we let Nut make money? Couldn't we use some jail-bird—some guy we don't have to pay?" Mr. Ratsky suggested, eagerly.

"The hanging of Nut," affirmed Mr. Wiseguy, "will be called an inspiration to every 'Forgotten Man,' 'Little Man,' 'Average Man' and all the unemployed fellows in this country. It will give them hope and cheer!"

"Tell me," protested Mr. Ratsky, "why this show has to be held in Union Square? Why not in Madison Square Garden? There are too many Reds, Socialists, Anarchists, and what not around Union Square." This was Mr. Ratsky's last protest.

"Just because," answered Mr. Wiseguy, calmly, "there are so many Reds, so many Socialists, so many Anarchists and so many 'What-Nots', that is why every atom of the air around Union Square and every inch of the ground have been deeply cursed! We must do something to clean the un-clean. Union Square is a historical spot. Our historical adventure must take place there!" While Mr. Wiseguy did his explaining he looked at the calendar.

"Mr. Wiseguy," said Mr. System, "I think there is too short a time in which to get things ready!"

"I'm going to use what's called American efficiency," replied Wiseguy. "In six days God made the world. In six days, we are going to remake the world! I saw Nut on Sunday night. At twelve o'clock this Saturday night we are going to complete our job of saving the world from becoming Bolshevized. Next Sunday, we are going to rest—just as God rests."

XXXIX:
"YOU CAN CALL ME BASTARD!"

"There is heat in the sun.
Vertically, at any time,
Horizontally, in any space,
Things must be done."

The whole building containing the Rich Men's Club was closely and secretly guarded.

Nut had the best teacher in town to teach him his dance steps—the preliminary Hanging Technique.

"I wish you all the good luck and success in the world, Mr. Nut," said the dance-instructress to him in a congratulatory tone. "I hope you will make lots of money by your hanging."

At this time, Mr. Wiseguy was resting on a sofa in the room.

Mr. Ratsky was snoring on another sofa.

Mr. System was watching.

The telephone rang.

Nut picked up the phone.

"This is the President of the North Atlantic Rope Corporation. We should like to offer the services of our ropes. We shall pay you the advertising fee at twice the New Deal rate."

"You bastard!" Nut hung up the phone.

The phone rang again. Nut answered it again.

"You call me a bastard when you are hanging and I'll pay you ten thousand dollars more."

"You bastard," Nut shouted laughingly.

"You should speak politely, Mr. Nut," said Mr. System. "Good Will Means Money!"

The phone rang. Nut took the call once more.

"Call from the Worst Suit Company. We have the latest Parisian Designs in Monkey Coats and Donkey Trousers! Our representative will be at your place any minute."

"Another advertising stunt!" exclaimed Nut. "Monkey Coats! Donkey Trousers!"

"A real Yankee you are!" said the dancing-instructress. And she approached Nut and held him tighter.

The phone rang again. Nut answered again.

"This is from the Roast Tobacco Company. Our offer is half a million dollars if you will smoke one of our cigarettes when you hang! Our representative will be down any minute!"

Again:

"This is from the Mild Tobacco Company. We will give you half a million and one cent. Our representative will be down any minute!"

Again:

"This is from the Real Tobacco Company. We will give you a half a million and one cent and a half. Our representative will be down any second!"

"I never smoked in my life," said Nut laughingly. "I don't need their cigarettes. And I don't care how much money they are going to give to me. And three companies . . ."

"When those guys come," said Mr. System, "we'll sign contracts with all of them." And Mr. System tapped the shoulder of Mr. Wiseguy, resting on the sofa. So Mr. Wiseguy began to teach Mr. Nut to smoke three cigarettes at a time—one in the left corner of his mouth, one in the right corner, and the third in the middle of his mouth.

Again the phone: Mr. Wiseguy answered it this time.

"This is the World Newspaper Syndicate calling. We want

Mr. Nut to write his autobiography in a hundred thousand words. It must be completed in forty-five minutes, so we can telegraph it to our papers throughout the world for immediate printing. Our representative will be down any minute!"

"It can't be done," replied Mr. Wiseguy. "The time is too short."

The Syndicate answered:

"We have plenty of autobiographies and biographies on hand. What we'll do is change the name Dog to Beast, or Cat to Rat. That is all."

Nut was still dancing. The dancing-instructress held him tighter and tighter.

"No matter how you do it, dearie," she said to Nut charmingly, "please mention my name—did I squeeze you, darling?—at your hanging. I am going to go into vaudeville and make one thousand dollars a week—Gee! Won't that be swell? Do you know Mrs. Diamond—Fifi to you!—Oh! Hold me tight!" the dance-instructress said as she squeezed him with all her might.

And because of her squeezing, the floor became wet—and smooth.

The phone rang: Mr. Nut took the call.

"I'm the president of the biggest institution of learning in the world. Because we are the biggest we are the best. The point of my words to you, however, nevertheless, is academically unacademic. May I have the honor of offering to you the highest degree of our Institution, Ph.D., L.L.B., M.M.C., Y.Y.Z.? If you can present our institution with an Endowment, we shall build a Nut Hall in which we shall teach the unemployed the trade of 'How to Hang Profitably.'"

The phone rang: Mr. System took the call.

"Is that you, Mr. System? Oh, thanks a great deal for thinking of me and sending me that complimentary stock in your Hanging Corporation. I will do anything I can in the Senate and House."

In the meantime Nut was getting along with his dancing nicely. Mr. Nut was acting nuttily. His eyes, however, were expressing deep thoughtfulness. He was acting nuttily as a soldier off for a war. But he was thoughtful as a soldier when he turns his gun.

The phone rang: Mr. System took the call.

"Mr. Nut, No, Dr. Nut! Telephone. A certain girl says, 'Comrade' and 'Class-conscious'! It must be that Communist, Stubborn."

Hearing the name "Stubborn" made Nut's face look different.

To be?

Or not to be?

To be.

When the dancing instructress heard Mr. System announce that "A certain girl is talking," she became a little bit jealous and she held Dr. Nut still tighter.

Mr. Wiseguy, hearing the announcement of Mr. System, jumped up and stopped Mr. Nut from using the phone. He took the receiver himself and said: "You Communist, Stubborn, go to hell, Stubborn!"

"Dr. Nut," said Mr. System suddenly, "hide yourself quickly! The newspaper reporters and Park Avenue ladies have broken in the door. You will be mobbed. Your body will be torn into pieces. And we shall have nothing to hang on Union Square!"

XL:

THE HANGING ON
UNION SQUARE

"There is heat in the sun.
Vertically, at any time,
Horizontally, in any space,
Things must be done!"

"For it is said that He will come." Now He was coming. And coming on that day.

The Flagpost in the center of the Square was arranged like the conning-tower of a battleship. The stage was three feet and nine inches from the top. The top of the Flagpost was green—like a Christmas tree on Christmas Day.

The stage was big enough to hold two people.

From the top of the Flagpost, a rope ran down. A loose knot was at the end of the rope.

The loose knot of the rope was one foot below the Stage.

Not only was radio apparatus attached to the stage, but also a television mechanism to enable the world to see Him.

And, surrounding the stage, things were so arranged that the members of Society who had come were able to see Him without using opera-glasses. And the places near the stage, according to the law of Supply and Demand, had by now become unobtainable.

It was going to be a dark night. Better so. For then in about the middle of the night the stars and Mars would arise in the East and illuminate the great event.

As the night would be dark, searchlights of three different colors and from three different directions were centered on the hanging spot. Light came from one searchlight on the Empire

State Building. Another searchlight was on the Tammany Hall Building and another atop the Riverside Church.[11] Business, Politics and the Holy Spirit formed a new Trinity.

On the Square, the cement pavement had been so treated that it was smooth and oily; and when the members of Society danced on it, Society's feet were keyed up and stimulated.

On the grassy spaces of the Square water-tanks were placed, so that the Square was a land and was a sea.

On the right side of the Flagpost was a stand for the diplomatic representatives of the Foreign Powers.

On the left side of the Flagpost was a stand for the Army and Navy Bands.

And, aloft, the motors and propellers of airplanes in curling motion, made a natural Air Band.

To the north and south of the Flagpost were seats for the editors of newspapers of the whole world, Russia excluded. Every detail of the hanging was to be studied and recorded.

The cheap buildings around the Square had become priceless and every inch of the territory in the Square was an inch of diamonds. For on this territory were the theater-boxes of Society, from which it could see the hanging.

Every entrance to the Square was gated. Each gate was in Napoleonic style.

But the finishing touch, and the best touch of the whole scene was the arrangement on top of the Flagpost. The last and highest touch was a Wheeling Dollar.

Across this Dollar Symbol were two mottos, namely:

> "The Dollar is Might!
> The Dollar is Right!"

There came the blessing of fair weather; it had been a soft and sunny day. The whole Saturday was in holiday spirit.

Everywhere one could hear:

> "Prosperity is coming back!
> Happy days are here again!"[12]

Fat, old, pearl-necked ladies were saying:

> *"He is coming! Our Lord!*
> *Amen!"*

At about ten o'clock all seats were taken in the Square.
Every street leading to the Square was packed.
Many persons had sandwiches in their overcoat-pockets.
Now came a parade. It was led by many and many bands.
The drums beat rhythmically:

> *"Go to the bank, go to the bank!*
> *Having money, you're in First Rank."*

On the sidewalks, children were screaming.
Women fainted.
"Here's a kiss!" a movie-crazy office-girl called. "Hello, Dr.
Nut."
"Isn't he cute? He's smiling," said another.
"We're with you! You're making money!" said still another.

At half-past eleven, Nut, led by Mr. System, Mr. Wiseguy, Mr.
Ratsky and Company, approached Union Square.

Nut was acting nuttily. His eyes, however, were expressing
deep thoughtfulness. He was acting nuttily as a soldier off
for a war. But he was thoughtful as a soldier when he turns
his gun.

They reached the base of the Flagpost.
All of Society rose. The bands played.

One step and then another, Mr. System and Mr. Nut ascended
the ladder to the top of the Stage.
Both Mr. System and Mr. Nut wore Monkey Coats and Don-
key Trousers.
"It is twelve o'clock Saturday night," Mr. Wiseguy announced!
"The Program will now begin!"

And now Mr. System spoke:

"Mr. God in Heaven, Ladies and Gentlemen on the Square, and Representatives of All Powers. Ladies and Gentlemen of the air:

"I, Mr. System, have the greatest pleasure in doing my duty towards saving this civilization!

"The unemployed of this country and of the world at large are day by day becoming more and more burdensome to our leading statesmen. The only way in which we can solve the problem of the unemployment is to hang all the unemployed. For otherwise they will suffer more.

"But this country is a land of freedom. And our philosophy is based on Individualism. And our motto is Profit for everybody. So today, a Forgotten Man, a Little Man, an Average Man, Mr. Nut, Dr. Nut, is doing his bit! Of his own free will, he is hanging himself on Union Square.

"His hanging is real. For he will really hang. No fake business here. Honesty is the best policy!

"What is more important is, that this hanging is a symbol. For it will give inspiration to the rest of the unemployed. And this hanging is also a challenge to the barbaric and savage system whose philosophy is based on Hate. Our system is based on Love!

"Since time is money, I now present our hero, a Forgotten Man, a Little Man, an Average Man! Dr. Nut. And finally I commend you to the Father of every family in Heaven and on Earth. God bless you all."

"Mr. System is a Shylock[13]—a Jew!"
    "May be or may not be a Jew: Mr. System—it must be you!"

"Bravo! Bravo! Hurray! Hurray!" shouted Society.
    "We want Dr. Nut!" yelled Society.
    "Speech! Speech! Speech!" was heard from all sides.

Overalls are coming!
    Unite! Fight!

———

"All right, but let him say only a few words," said Mr. Wise-guy to Mr. System. "Our people like action."

Nut now spoke:

"I am a Forgotten Man, a Little Man, an Average Man, a Worker, a Nut.
  "'Be good and starve is the order of the day!
  "'Prey on others or become a prey!'
  "I *was* a Nut. But I *am* a Nut no more.
  "I, a Forgotten Man, a Little Man, an Average Man, a Worker—will this time—double-cross you, Mr. System—the Exploiter, the War-maker, the Man-killer.
  "Here is your neck. This is your rope."

Nut turned his gun.
  Nut double-crossed Mr. System.

THE END

Afterword

"The Trouble Maker." So signed off H. T. Tsiang—writer, actor, and agitator—in a letter to artist-activist Rockwell Kent on January 15, 1941. By this point in Tsiang's career, such a moniker was more than justified.[1] Born in rural China, he had vigorously advocated against Japanese imperialism; fled into exile in the U.S. after breaking with his political party; founded a newspaper to promote a leftist agenda; led protests in California; spent time in jail for disturbing the peace; escaped to New York City; published five books, all of which, in one way or another, advocated for world revolution after the Soviet model; and was at that very moment sitting in a cell at the Ellis Island detention center awaiting possible deportation, ostensibly for overstaying his student visa, but perhaps also for promoting anarchy.[2]

Throughout this whirlwind of political and creative activity, Tsiang always continued to write, sometimes using toilet paper when no other material was available. During just the time he was at Ellis Island, he wrote letters to politicians, appeals for help from organizations like the ACLU, a series of narrative poems, and many shorter works. (Two of his most memorable lines from this period—"Statue, turn your ass! / Let us pass!"—were addressed to the Statue of Liberty in reference to that icon's literal and figurative stance toward Ellis Island detainees.[3])

Tsiang had lofty ambitions for his writings; he believed they could lay bare truths about social conditions that would inspire readers to change them. Although he may never have met James Baldwin, who also spent time in Greenwich Village in the 1930s, he would undoubtedly have agreed with Baldwin's view that "You write in order to change the world, knowing perfectly well that you probably can't, but also knowing that literature is indispensable to the world. The world changes according to the way people see it, and if you alter, even but a millimeter, the way people look at reality, then you can change it."[4] As the protagonist in Tsiang's first novel, *China Red,* declares: "With our paper bullets, we shall change the direction of the wind" (90).

Among his many paper bullets, Tsiang singled out *The Hanging on Union Square* as worthy of sharing with Rockwell Kent, whom he fondly dubbed "My dear Mr. Hell-Raiser." In Kent, Tsiang discovered a sympathetic reader who understood the subtlety of his work like few others. Kent was known not only as an accomplished painter and printmaker (his illustrations for *Moby-Dick* contributed to the popularity of the book's re-issue) but also as a socialist and lecturer on topics such as "art for the people."[5] Although the two had never met in person, Kent generously agreed to review Tsiang's case and writings. He wrote encouragingly to Tsiang:

> It is no reflection upon the serious nature of your political thought and the serious underlying intention of "The Hanging on Union Square" to say that in reading it aloud, as we are doing, we are in constant laughter. You have delightful humor and every bit of it is sharply pointed. Beyond this, we find your work very moving.[6]

Two weeks later, when Kent and his wife finished reading the novel, they agreed that "it held us absorbed and moved until the very end. It is an extraordinary book."[7]

Other contemporary reviewers who caught the humor of Tsiang's book often presumed it to be the result of simplicity rather than political guile. Eda Lou Walton, writing for the *New York Herald Tribune,* found Tsiang's novel "amusing" but assumed that "the Chinese author is naïve, not desperate and hard-boiled. When he talks of flop-houses, of street life, of perversions, he does so with true Chinese reticence. Because the reader knows perfectly just what is going on, the author's euphemisms become terribly funny."[8] Kenneth White came closer to the mark in his review for the *New Republic*, explaining that "the brutal gaiety of the book, the intentionally naïve humor, gain it more effectiveness than might be found in a dozen soggy novels about the same situations."[9] Tsiang confided to Kent that he had intentionally lightened his tone "so as to keep many Liberal Minded and serious persons with us," but Tsiang's wild mash up of methods and moods confused both Walton and White.[10] "What is any critic to do with a man who so completely mixes up Chinese symbols and American slang, fantasy and complete seriousness?" asks Walton in her review. Meanwhile, White questioned whether *The Hanging on Union Square* was "more a cartoon than a novel."

More than eighty years after the book appeared on the streets of New York City, hand sold by Tsiang himself, these questions still remain. With its idiosyncratic mix of narrative, poetic, and dramatic conventions; American, Chinese, and Soviet models; and humor and seriousness, *The Hanging on Union Square* is an audacious, *sui generis* satire—the literary equivalent of outsider art, but one with deeply political intentions. What are we to make of such a work? What is any critic to do?

TSIANG'S JOURNEY FROM CHINA TO UNION SQUARE

Although it is never a good idea to conflate an author with one of his fictional creations, Tsiang himself was not averse to identifying himself with Mr. Nut, the main hero and chief Trouble Maker of *The Hanging on Union Square*. In a scathing letter to FDR's secretary, Stephen Early, written on May 30, 1941, just six months before the bombing of Pearl Harbor, Tsiang berates the administration for selling weapons to Japan: "You Americans sold Japanese irons and build up Japanese battleships but now feel sorry and try to catch up. Too late."[11] Tsiang then warns Early not to underestimate him:

[T]he one who thinks that I may [be] worth no more than a
Nut to the Chinese people is a jackass. A Nut cannot and dare
not write you this letter. Ah, so I am dangerous and I am the
one that must be deported, even use the punch delivered below
the belt. . . . I present my own rope: to intern me! Well, well,
that's Nut talking! Nuts to you.

The story of how Tsiang came to think of himself as someone with Nut-like qualities begins in China. Tsiang was born in
1899 to poor, working-class parents in Qi'an, a village in the
district of Nantong, Jiangsu Province. His father, a grain-store
worker, and his mother, a maid, both died young. According to
his sister, Songzhen, Tsiang was such an excellent student that
he was able to earn scholarships to the Tongzhou Teachers'
School in Jiangsu and Southeastern University in Nanjing,
where he learned English and studied political economics.[12]

Tsiang seems to have been a rabble-rouser from an early
age. During school breaks, he advocated against ancestral
worship and foot binding as antiquated and unjust practices;
and when the Chinese government agreed to Japan's humiliat-
ing Twenty-One Demands (including ceding control of lands
and other resources), Tsiang organized a protest movement in
his hometown.

Like other reform-minded Chinese, Tsiang found an inspirational leader in Sun Yat-sen, known as the father of the Chinese
independence movement. In particular, he approved of Sun's
willingness to work with communists in both the Soviet Union
and China.[13] After graduating from Southeastern University,
Tsiang took a position as one of Sun's secretaries in the Kuomintang (KMT) or Nationalist Party. After Sun's death, however,
the party split between two opposing groups: one led by Liao
Zhongkai that was interested in cooperating with the Chinese
Communist Party against the common foe of Japan; and one
that veered towards a more conservative, anti-communist
agenda, spearheaded by Chiang Kai-shek. Tsiang threw in his
lot with Liao and his faction. In fact, Tsiang was accompanying
Liao to a KMT Executive Committee meeting on August 30,
1925 when the latter was assassinated. Believing that he, too,

faced the "executioner's axe" for his leftist allegiance, Tsiang attempted to flee to the Soviet Union. When that plan proved impractical, he left for the United States instead.[14]

In 1926, Tsiang enrolled at Stanford University. This allowed him to circumvent the Chinese Exclusion Act of 1882, which prevented "Chinese laborers" from entering the country but gave an exemption for students. While based in California, Tsiang founded a bilingual periodical, the *Chinese Guide in America*, which sought to inform a broader audience about the political situation in China and the need for worldwide revolution.

Alas, some Californians were less than sympathetic to Tsiang's political beliefs. In 1927, a mob attacked him as he was distributing leaflets critical of the Chinese government. On February 26, 1928, police raided the Los Angeles headquarters of the leftist wing of the KMT and arrested "H. T. Tsiang, said to be the leader of the radicals" prior to a demonstration that he had been planning against a leader of the conservative wing of the party who was visiting from China.[15] After his release, Tsiang relocated to New York, where he enrolled at Columbia University and sought new opportunities to enact social change. Tsiang's Columbia transcript tells us that he took classes from 1928 until 1930. While there, Tsiang received special encouragement from Professors Mark Van Doren and Ashley Thorndike.[16] In his new East Coast milieu, Tsiang also made the acquaintance of leftist writers such as Mike Gold, Langston Hughes, and Parker Tyler.

Given the intellectual environment at the time, it's not surprising that the focus of Tsiang's political work shifted from journalism and organizing to poetry. According to literary critic Cary Nelson, writing poetry had, by the 1920s and 1930s, become "a credible form of revolutionary action" in the U.S.[17] Tsiang began publishing poems about the political situation in China and the working conditions of Chinese Americans in the U.S., several of which appeared in 1928 in the *Daily Worker* and *New Masses*. He went on to self-publish his first book, *Poems of the Chinese Revolution*, in 1929. This initial effort was followed by four other books: three novels—*China Red* (1931), *The Hanging on Union Square* (1935), and

And China Has Hands (1937)—as well as one play, *China Marches On* (1938).

While Tsiang may have been idiosyncratic in many ways, he certainly developed his style in the context of like-minded writers. Historians inform us that the cafeterias in the Union Square neighborhood were "well-known sites for both queer and leftist gatherings."[18] By 1931, Tsiang had moved from Columbia University to an area near Union Station and had become an active participant in leftist writing communities.[19] Sam Bluefarb, who frequented the Life Cafeteria on nearby Sheridan Square, describes it as "a popular hangout for artists, writers, bohemians, and a mixed bag of cranks and eccentrics," where the "coffee-drinking, the smoking, the talk would drone on into the small hours of morning." Bluefarb observes that Tsiang was a "recognizable character who frequented the cafeteria." According to this account at least, Tsiang would work quietly in a corner writing and revising *The Hanging on Union Square*, which Bluefarb reports, "was popular with many of us at the time."[20] Eventually, however, Tsiang seems to have annoyed others with his persistent attempts to promote his agenda and his work. A *New Masses* editorial published on August 27, 1935 describes how Tsiang "made himself a familiar, and now unwelcome figure, at radical gatherings where he sells his books."[21]

Tsiang's cafeteria perch and presence at leftist gatherings and on the streets between Columbia University, Broadway, and Greenwich Village would have given him ample opportunity to witness the impact that the Great Depression had on his fellow New Yorkers. Likewise, his stint as a dishwasher at the Howdy Club in Greenwich Village—a place known for its risqué burlesque performances—might very well have supplied him with inspiration for Miss Digger's memorable stage appearance, in addition to giving him personal experience with the conditions of a manual laborer living on the edge of subsistence.[22] Whatever his source material may have been, it's clear that Tsiang hoped to find a broad audience for *The Hanging on Union Square*; in 1941, he spoke with an editor at Random House, claiming that among all of his works, *Hanging* is "The Best Horse that you can bet on."[23]

Interestingly, in spite of the fact that H. T. Tsiang played Mr. Nut in dramatic adaptations of *The Hanging on Union Square*[24]—and despite his clear and deep involvement with issues of race and specifically China in his previous works—the novel never marks Mr. Nut as Chinese or even Chinese American. The plight of immigrant Chinese workers in New York had been the subject of Tsiang's early poem, "Chinaman, Laundryman"—and later his novel *And China Has Hands*—but *Hanging* employs as its protagonist a racially unspecified (though easily read as white) Everyman figure. At the beginning of *The Hanging on Union Square*, Mr. Nut finds himself trapped by his inability to pay his cafeteria bill: "A ten-cent check. A nickel in my pocket—I'm in Hell." That quandary, more than race or background, marks out the parameters of Mr. Nut's existence; like many others during the Depression, Mr. Nut has recently lost his job and is struggling to survive. We never learn what his former occupation might have been. All we know is that he once harbored middle-class aspirations.

Why did Tsiang turn from writing about Chinese politics in his 1929 *Poems of the Chinese Revolution* and his 1931 novel, *China Red,* to this 1935 novel featuring an ethnically unmarked protagonist navigating Depression-era Manhattan? What did this change of setting and subject matter mean for Tsiang as a writer? What is the significance of Union Square as the site of the novel's climax? Alas, Tsiang left no known papers or descendants to suggest definitive answers.

Perhaps it is enough to say simply that Tsiang wrote what he knew in 1935, as he had in his earlier books.[25] Alternatively, Tsiang may have had more strategic reasons for his choice of subject matter. While Mr. Nut finds himself trapped in a monetary predicament, H. T. Tsiang may have felt trapped by his identity as a "young Chinese poet." No less a personage than Upton Sinclair once wrote of Tsiang that "This is a voice to which the white world . . . will have to listen more and more as time passes. I do not mean to this particular young Chinese poet, but to the movement which he voices."

Although his racialized and national identities might very well have been his entrée to the New York leftist community, perhaps Tsiang, like many other ethnic American authors, felt burdened by this expectation to represent. Or perhaps he believed that readers had difficulty generalizing from his specific examples. He clearly makes the case in "Chinaman, Laundryman" that all workers of the world, regardless of race, need to unite, but perhaps his readers had difficulty reading beyond their expectations—especially since the argument appears in a book entitled *Poems of the Chinese Revolution.*[26] In writing *The Hanging on Union Square,* then, Tsiang may have been attempting to escape the confines of his audience's expectations and his own narrowly defined identity.

Locating the main action of the novel in and around Union Square, rather than China or Chinatown, might likewise signal Tsiang's desire to participate in a broader political and historical conversation. Situated at the junction of Broadway and Fourth Avenue, Union Square, named for the union of these two major thoroughfares (though the streets themselves once had different names), came to serve as a rallying point for all kinds of civic demonstrations in New York City. After the Confederacy attacked Fort Sumter, initiating the Civil War, huge crowds gathered at the foot of George Washington's statue there to rally for national unity. The first official Labor Day parade took place there. And throughout the early twentieth century, advocates for both patriotism and protest made Union Square their stage, whether to celebrate the Declaration of Independence or to protest the convictions of Julius and Ethel Rosenberg. Smaller gatherings and individual soap-box orators also made use of Union Square.[27] This was a place from which one could address not only New York, but the whole of the United States, and perhaps even the world—and Tsiang claimed it in his 1935 novel.

REVOLUTIONIZING THE REPRESENTATION OF REALITY

To say that *The Hanging on Union Square* does not operate stylistically in the realm of conventional realism might seem like something of an understatement, despite the fact that Tsiang sets his novel in what is recognizably New York in the 1930s. Like other contemporary leftist writers of his day, Tsiang believed that realistic fiction reinforced a capitalist view of the world, one that seemed to suggest that individuals primarily determined their fate in the context of a free market.

In the author's note appended to the end of Waldo Frank's foreword to the book, Tsiang explains that, in writing *Hanging*, he "employed the method of 'Socialistic Realism and Revolutionary Romanticism.'" Socialist Realism, described by Russian writer and theorist Maxim Gorky as an antidote to "bourgeois realism," was originally theorized as a way for literature to help shape the ideological foundations of the Soviet state.[28] But while different writers interpreted Gorky's ideas in varying ways, most understood "the socialist-realist perception of the world not as something already formed and petrified but in terms of progress and development."[29] Tsiang, too, represents reality as dynamic in *Hanging*. Depression-era New York includes groups relating to one another in tension and flux: some are trying to "save" capitalism, others are merely surviving, still others are preying upon those trying to survive. And a few are working towards revolution. Hence, his novel not only represents everyday reality, but also offers a critical and unsettled view of it.

Similarly, revolutionary romanticism sought to dispel false, lulling beliefs in the oppressive, bourgeois status quo, striving instead to reveal a new path for the working classes. As Moissaye Olgin explains in a 1934 article for *New Masses*, a magazine that Tsiang avidly read, "revolutionary romanticism" is:

> romanticism that forecasts the future, that sees the outlines of a future beautiful life in the present struggles of the workers, a romanticism which combines a sober attitude towards the present with an understanding of the tremendous changes in life and the human personality that will take place under proletarian rule.[30]

As Olgin's explanation makes clear, revolutionary romanticism emphasizes the systemic changes in store for the group rather than possibilities for the kind of individual fulfillment typically associated with conventional romanticism.

In *Hanging*, Tsiang references the conventions of traditional realism and bourgeois romance but gives them the ideological spin described by Gorky and Olgin. It should thus come as no surprise that Tsiang is not trying for subtlety in his depiction of how dominant financial, governmental, and religious interests—"a new Trinity" formed by "Business, Politics and the Holy Spirit"—all fail, and often outright exploit, the weak and vulnerable. Characters display hardly any psychological depth, and the novel's "plot" develops in a herky-jerky, seemingly irrational way.

In this way, the novel makes us understand that politics and economics have more to do with Mr. Nut and Miss Stubborn's relationship than anything we might call love. Although Mr. Nut's near-love-connection with Miss Stubborn helps to propel the novel's narrative, he ultimately comes to understand that Miss Stubborn, the most clearly identified communist in the novel, is more important as a political exemplar than as a potential mate. Likewise, Miss Digger is a distraction, though of a different sort and with a different purpose. In the end, the novel makes us understand that the "future beautiful life" of Mr. Nut and Miss Stubborn lies not in marital bliss or bourgeois domesticity but in a wider class-based revolution. Consequently, *Hanging* ends not with the guy getting the girl but rather with Mr. Nut as a fully transformed class-conscious hero who uses his apparent naiveté to lead Mr. System into a trap. As the novel's narrator intones more than once:

> Nut was acting nuttily. His eyes, however, were expressing
> deep thoughtfulness. He was acting nuttily as a soldier off for
> war. But he was thoughtful as a soldier when he turns his gun.

This insistence on the disruption of traditional novelistic technique in the service of political messaging puts *Hanging* squarely in league with a form that would eventually come to be known as the "collective novel." According to literary historian Barbara Foley, collective novels employ "experimental devices that break up the narrative and rupture the illusion of seamless transparency."³¹ Certainly, *Hanging*'s lack of seamless plotlines and often jarring juxtapositions of poetry and prose, humor and seriousness, performance and exposition, seem to qualify it as an example of the form.

In addition, collective novels feature the collective or "the group as a phenomenon greater than—and different from— the sum of the individuals who constitute it" and "narratorial interventions [that] unambiguously remind readers that they should conceive of the characters as a unified group." Thus, while we might think that we know people as individuals, Tsiang's novel jarringly reminds us that we often overlook the specificity of fellow human beings and reduce them to types: a nut, a gold-digger, a stubborn communist, a rat-like gangster, and a capitalist. Tsiang's novel goes on to group Mr. System, Mr. Wiseguy, and Mr. Ratsky as members of the "Rich Men's Club," which schemes together at the "Conference for Saving Capitalism." Opposing them are Mr. Nut, Miss Digger, and Miss Stubborn, who eventually realize their common class interests, though their group identity never gets dramatized as clearly as the Rich Men's Club.

Another characteristic of collective novels is, as Foley explains, that they "frequently assert direct documentary links with the world of the reader" by presenting "verisimilitudinous descriptions of environment" and making "unambiguous reference to verifiable episodes in the class struggle."³² Tsiang's novel accomplishes this documentary function by describing Mr. Nut's perambulations through mid-1930s Manhattan street by street, naming particular landmarks and referring to events such as the suicide of artist Gan Kolski on April 18, 1932 and the attempted assassination of President Franklin D. Roosevelt by Giuseppe Zangara on February 15, 1933. Interestingly, then, the effectiveness of the collective novel turns on its ability to invoke a sense of everyday reality at the same time that it disrupts it in key ways.

Some of Tsiang's inspiration for these techniques—and indeed for the book as a whole—might very well have been the 1933 novel *Union Square* by Albert Halper, described by Foley as one of the best examples of the collective novel. Like *Hanging*, Halper's book also features a perambulating protagonist who meets characters named for particular aspects of their identity, such as Mr. Boardman, a manufacturing executive, and Mr. Feibleman, a relatively powerless vendor of toasted chestnuts. While both Halper's and Tsiang's novels follow collective novel conventions, however, the latter experiments with them more freely, mixing them with ideas from other forms.

Another, related genre of radical literature from which Tsiang undoubtedly borrowed was the agitprop play, a significant part of the New York theater scene of the 1930s. Unlike conventional plays, which invited audiences to identify with individualized characters facing and resolving crises in typically realistic settings, agitprop plays discouraged audience identification and traditional expectations regarding plot. In 1931, when director and playwright Hallie Flanagan first observed such theatre, "she discerned the start of a distinct theatrical and dramaturgical style consisting of 'a direct, terse, hard-hitting phraseology, a machine gun repetition, [and] a sharp, type analysis with no individual characterization.'"[33] Plays in this style sought to alert audiences to the ideological blinders that they wore. And by encouraging their viewers to see the world anew, they hoped to push them to take action. To accomplish this, agitprop plays employed various alienating effects including harsh sounds and lighting, stylized movement, direct addresses to the audience, and dialogue filled with non sequiturs, in addition to the kind of linguistic repetition described by Flanagan.

Tsiang knew well the world of the agitprop play, having acted in *Roar China* in 1930,[34] so it is unsurprising that many of its conventions pop up in *Hanging*. Like a play, Tsiang's novel is divided into four acts. It also self-consciously includes terse, repetitive language that aims not at telling a traditional story but rather at revealing a critical perspective on reality and calling audience members to action. At the beginning of the novel—and in the first three acts in the book—we read the following words:

It's under this system!
It's under this system!

Mr. System
Beware:
The Hanging
On
Union Square! . . .

These lines read very much like a script for a mass recitation, an agitprop form that "consisted of a simple descriptive narrative, often a poem, that built to a direct exhortation of the audience, normally to organize, strike, or fight."[35]

So while some critics may have misunderstood Tsiang's repetitive language as a humorous indication of his naiveté or a lack of fluency in English, we can recognize it as being motivated by a sharp political mind that asks us to think even as we smile at sequences such as: "He is radical; he has no money. He is conservative; he has money. He is wishy-washy; he has a wishy-washy amount of money." Just as a crowd at the end of the novel chants and follows searchlights to the stage at the center of Union Square, we, the readers of this novelized version of agitprop, are asked to think about material and social conditions "under this system." We are being asked to move ideologically from our initial, unwitting gathering for the purposes of entertainment to Mr. Nut's ultimate, if implicit, call to join not just a revolutionary way of seeing reality, but also a revolution itself.[36]

AN EPIC SATIRE

As readers, we experience this critical, dynamic version of reality not only by traveling along Tsiang's stylistically bumpy road, but also from the perspective of Mr. Nut—and in particular, his journey from false consciousness to class consciousness. Given this political trajectory, it comes as no surprise that Tsiang chose to subtitle his novel "An American Epic."[37] Like James Joyce, whose 1922 modernist classic *Ulysses* featured a similarly perambulating hero and chapters pegged to the hours of the day, Tsiang may have hoped that associating his novel with the genre of the epic would help to suggest the global and momentous importance of his relatively local and mundane narrative.

As with all epics, *Hanging* begins *in medias res,* in this instance with Mr. Nut not being able to pay his ten-cent check. And although Mr. Nut is neither favored by Athena nor gifted with cleverness or martial prowess, Tsiang's hero does possess some special qualities that belie his humble exterior and unemployed status. For example, despite his basic innocence, he is observant and broadly empathetic.

This becomes apparent very early on, when he first meets Miss Stubborn, whom he initially takes to be a young man. Trying to make conversation, he asks: "How's business?" Immediately, the narrator reports from Mr. Nut's perspective:

> Upon hearing this, the color of the young fellow's face suddenly changed and his eyebrows rose. The dark spots of his eyes became steady and because of the steadiness it made the surrounding white parts appear smaller. Mr. Nut knew that the young fellow was angry. But Mr. Nut didn't know why.

Mr. Nut proves throughout the narrative to be generous, thoughtful, and in the end, resolute. This makes him a fine hero in a Marxist epic, for it enables us to watch a fairly likable character observe and interact with other people, with and against whom he will work to gain a truer sense of the world and his role in it. At one level, *Hanging* is about a day in the life of one unemployed man, but the epic conventions encourage us to expect more.

Such moves were familiar to those who, like Tsiang, aspired to be practitioners of Socialist Realism. As literary critic Katerina Clark explains, novels in this tradition typically follow a central character as he or she undergoes a rite of passage, which normally involves a journey to consciousness, consultation with mentors, distractions, sacrifice, crises, and a climax that marks the character's transformation.[38] Thus Mr. Nut is introduced to us as a cog recently ejected from the capitalist machine, having lost his job three months before the start of the novel. In Act I, he finds himself in the awkward position of not being able to pay his bill at a cafeteria. In spite of his commonality with the dispossessed, Mr. Nut at first clings to the bourgeois ideology of upward mobility:

> Yes, he was a worker. Now. For the time being! But how could they tell that he would not, someday, by saving some money, establish a business of his own?

In short, Mr. Nut begins with false consciousness and hence perceives reality through false—i.e., conventional or bourgeois—eyes. He undertakes a journey, learns from others, descends into the Underworld (via a movie theater), offers to sacrifice himself, overcomes obstacles, and ultimately perceives reality and those around him in a "truer," more critical way. This journey both educates Mr. Nut about the kinds of desperation faced by his fellow city-dwellers, and reveals the exploitation that the powerful exercise on the weak. By the end, he understands that Mr. Wiseguy was never his friend, Mr. System has to be taken down, and Miss Stubborn is not only attractive but also correct.

If the clear purpose of all of Tsiang's literary appropriation was political change, his radical ambitions are apparent from the very first—in fact, from the original edition's extremely unconventional cover, which reads: "YES . . . the cover of a book / is more of a book / than the book is a book . . . I say—NO . . . SO." By proclaiming the fact of *Hanging*'s publication-as-a-book as opposed to a collection of loose manuscript pages, the cover works simultaneously as boast and critique: boast on behalf of the author's tenacity and critique of those who do not value his ideas.

To these notions, Tsiang says both "yes" and "no." Yes, the book is now available for dissemination and hence has a different kind of value than a sheaf of typewritten paper. But no, the ideas between the covers are not in and of themselves any more valuable than if they had not been bound. Of course, a major theme in *Hanging* concerns covers or appearances. Mr. Wiseguy thinks that elevator shoes make the man, and most dismiss Mr. Nut as a harmless fool based on his appearance. But it turns out in the end that Mr. Wiseguy is as short on mettle as Mr. Nut is dangerous.

So when Tsiang opens his tale in classic epic fashion with an invocation to the muses, it's an invocation with a twist. Instead of calling on immortal beings for inspiration, he locates the authority of the muse in himself:

> What is unsaid
> Says,
> And says more
> Than what is said.
>
> SAYS I

With characteristic humor and seeming illogic, even the authority of self-as-muse is undercut by the message of the invocation itself. Tsiang's "American epic" features a muse that asks us to constantly question appearances and listen to silences. Much remains unsaid in conventional realism and bourgeois society; what remains unspoken is often more valuable than what is spoken. Like the burlesque shows at the Howdy Club, *The Hanging on Union Square* proceeds to both hide and reveal its significance.

From his early days protesting against foot-binding to his short political career working for Sun Yat-sen to his later days advocating for economic justice, Tsiang aimed to move people to action through his writings—paper bullets that could change the direction of the wind. With *The Hanging on Union Square*, Tsiang put his oar into the conversation about what was wrong with the world during the 1930s. He wanted to transcend his identity as a "young Chinese poet" and become a major troublemaker, an idiosyncratic, hybrid version of Hamlet, Odysseus, Christ, and his own fictional creation, Mr. Nut.[39] And he sought to achieve this purpose by imaginatively—and perhaps indiscriminately—borrowing techniques from a dizzying variety of genres. In so doing, Tsiang may have been following the principle of *nalai zhuyi,* or strategic appropriation from other writers, formulated by the influential Chinese author and literary theorist Lu Xun.[40] Lu argued that globalism and modernism compelled writers to abandon notions of generic purity; he thus encouraged writers to accomplish their artistic—and sometimes political—ends by freely appropriating from a variety of sources. Even Lu, however, may not have been able to predict the creative and disorienting ways that *The Hanging on Union Square* combines these forms.

Small wonder then that every publisher Tsiang initially approached declined to take on *The Hanging on Union Square.* Putnam's Sons, Minton, Balch, & Company could not imagine that the book would sell well enough to make "publication remunerative." Little, Brown, & Company and Coward-McCann agreed. Covici-Friede suggested that he "re-write the story in straight-forward terms as a realistic novel." Of course, H. T. Tsiang did not aim for remuneration or realism. Thanks to his own initiative, people were able to read his book during his lifetime. Thanks to Penguin Classics, the Trouble Maker's masterwork will find the mainstream audience he always sought.

FLOYD CHEUNG

NOTES

1. All Tsiang-Rockwell correspondence can be found in the Rockwell Kent papers at the Archives of American Art, Smithsonian Institution. In all of Tsiang's publications, he signed his name as H. T. Tsiang. His full name on official documents is Hsi-tseng Tsiang. The Library of Congress romanizes his family name as Chiang, and in the pinyin system, his full name is Jiang Xizeng.

2. Besides being in possible violation of the Chinese Exclusion Act of 1882, Tsiang may have faced deportation under the Alien Immigration Act of 1917 and the Anarchist Act of 1918, which sought to exclude radical and subversive aliens.

3. For this and other compositions, his fellow inmate Pierre Ferrand called Tsiang the "Poet Laureate of Ellis Island." See *A Question of Allegiance* (Tampa: American Studies Press, 1990), 73–75.

4. James Baldwin, interview by Mel Watkins, *New York Times Book Review* (23 Sep. 1979): 3.

5. Qtd. from the biographical note accompanying the Rockwell Kent papers.

6. Letter from Kent to Tsiang, 14 Jan. 1941.

7. Letter from Kent to Tsiang, 30 Jan. 1941. Kent and his wife would eventually regret reaching out to Tsiang on account of his annoying persistence.

8. Rev. of *The Hanging on Union Square. New York Herald Tribune* 9 June. 1935: 9.

9. Rev. of *The Hanging on Union Square. New Republic* 31 July 1935: 343–44.

10. Letter from Tsiang to Kent, 17 Jan. 1941. I have preserved most of Tsiang's idiosyncratic capitalizations and grammar in my quotations from his letters.

11. Letter from Tsiang to Stephen Early, 30 May 1941, Rockwell Kent Papers.

12. Jiang, Songzhen. "Meiyou wangji de qinren [An Unforgettable Relative]." *Dushu [Reading]* 12 (1983): 142. I am indebted to Lu Li for translation assistance.

13. Of course, Sun's biographers differ on the degree to which such communist collaboration was strategic.

14. In his preface to Tsiang's *Poems,* Upton Sinclair described Tsiang as "a young Chinese student whom the American authorities sought to deport and deliver to the executioner's axe at home."

15. "Chinese Meet Peacefully," *Los Angeles Times* 27 Feb. 1928: A9. ProQuest Historical Newspapers.

16. Thanks to Columbia University archivist Jocelyn Wilk for her assistance in confirming that Tsiang took Thorndike's English 241: The Life and Work of Shakespeare. Tsiang acknowledges Van Doren and Thorndike in his foreword to his *Poems.*

17. Cary Nelson, "Poetry Chorus: Dialogic Politics in 1930s Poetry" in *Radical Revisions: Rereading 1930s Culture,* ed., Bill Mullen and Sherry Lee Linkon (Urbana: U of Illinois P, 1996), 32.

18. Aaron Lecklider, "H. T. Tsiang's Proletarian Burlesque: Performance and Perversion in *The Hanging on Union Square*," *MELUS* 36.4 (2011): 87–113. See also, George Chauncey, *Gay New York: Gender, Urban Culture, and the Making of the Gay Male World 1890–1940* (New York: Basic, 1994).

19. He listed Box 66 in Station D, New York City as his mailing address at this time. Station D was located at the corner of 4th Avenue and East 13th Street, according to the New York City directory.

20. Sam Bluefarb, "Notes from a Memoir," *New English Review* (Sep. 2011), <http://www.newenglishreview.org/custpage.cfm/96357/sec_id/96357>.

21. "Between Ourselves," *New Masses,* 27 Aug. 1935: 30.

22. See "Howdy Club," Lost Womyn's Space, <http://lostwomyns space.blogspot.com/2011/08/howdy-club.html>. For an illuminating discussion of Tsiang's work as a proletarian burlesque, see Lecklider.

23. Letter from Tsiang to Shirley Johnstone, 7 Sep. 1941, Rockwell Kent Papers.

24. He later went on to adapt the novel for the stage while studying at Erwin Piscator's Dramatic Workshop at the New School for Social Research in New York City and later in Los Angeles. Theatre critic Katherine Von Blon reported on Tsiang's production of *Hanging* twice in Los Angeles. In 1944, she raved that the one-act version of the play was "lit by the passion of genuine poetry." Von Blon also understood Tsiang's "mingled technique of the Chinese and American, with a touch of Stanislavsky." In 1948, Von Blon praised Tsiang as an actor, who by this time was "well known for his Oriental characterizations in films" such as *The Purple Heart* (1944), *The Keys of the Kingdom* (1944), and *Black Gold* (1947). She wrote that *Hanging* "still remains a gleaming satire, lit by the lamp of rich philosophy," and "Tsiang again scored as the hapless little Mr. Nut."

25. From 1926 to 1931, he published the *Chinese Guide* and wrote about Chinese political turmoil; he had just escaped being assassinated and sought to continue his advocacy from his new base in America.

26. Floyd Cheung, "Tsiang's 'Chinaman, Laundryman,'" *Explicator* 61.4 (2003): 226–29.

27. See Joanna Merwood-Salisbury, "Patriotism and Protest: Union Square as Public Space, 1832–1932," *Journal of the Society of Architectural Historians* 68.4 (2009): 540–59.

28. The 1934 Union of Soviet Writers, led by Maxim Gorky, discussed the role of Socialist Realism in the ideological shaping of the Soviet state, and agreed upon the following: "Active participation of Soviet writers, by means of their artistic writing, in building socialism, defense of the interests of the working class, and securing the role of Soviets through true representations of the class struggle and socialist construction in our country, and through the education of the working class in the spirit of socialism." "Soviet Literature" in *Problems of Soviet Literature: Reports and Speeches at the First Soviet Writers' Congress,* H. G. Scott, ed. (London: M. Lawrence, 1935), 42.

29. Piotr Fast, *Ideology, Aesthetics, Literary History: Socialist Realism and Its Others* (Frankfurt: Peter Lang, 1999), 40.

30. "A Pageant of Soviet Literature," *New Masses* (Oct. 1934): 17–18.

31. Barbara Foley, *Radical Representations: Politics and Form in U.S. Proletarian Fiction, 1929–1941* (Durham: Duke UP, 1993), 400–2.

32. Ibid., 400.

33. Regine Robin, *Socialist Realism: An Impossible Aesthetic,* trans. Catherine Porter (Stanford: Stanford UP, 1992), 93.

34. Translated into English from the Russian by F. Polianovska and Barbara Nixon, *Roar China* recounts the oppression of the Chinese by Western imperial powers who exploit, abuse, and eventually kill those who stand in the way of their profit and control. At the conclusion of the play, a British naval officer orders the hanging of two Chinese boatmen, after which a crowd of angry Chinese "roar" their disapproval. Tsiang played the 2nd Boatman out of four. This theatrical hanging may thus have inspired the hanging at the end of his novel.

   Tsiang would eventually go on to write, produce, and act in his own agitprop-influenced plays including *China Marches On, Canton Rickshaw,* and *Wedding at a Nudist Colony.* In the 1940s, he studied with Erwin Piscator, who along with Bertholt Brecht, theorized and popularized agitprop theatre.

35. Robin, 89.

36. On January 6, 1935, the New York Civic Theater's production of *Waiting for Lefty* by Clifford Odets famously succeeded in inciting a protest. According to Colette Hyman, the play stirred its audience to such an extent that they "jumped onto the stage[,] poured into the street," and began a labor demonstration. See Colette Hyman, *Staging Strikes: Workers' Theatre and the American Labor Movement* (Philadelphia: Temple UP, 1997), 1.

37. The idea of a reconceived or rewritten epic must have resonated with Tsiang in more ways than one: Tsiang writes in his author's note to *Hanging* that he is in the process of writing a book called "Shanghai-New York-Moscow: An Odyssey of a Chinese Coolie," and his professor at Columbia, Ashley Thorndike, believed that writers of every generation ought to adapt established models to suit their specific situations, each one creating "a new *Odyssey*." See Ashley Thorndike, *The Outlook for Literature* (New York: Macmillan, 1931), 69.

38. Katerina Clark, *The Soviet Novel: History as Ritual*, 3rd ed. (Bloomington: Indiana UP, 2000), 167.

39. Like Hamlet, Mr. Nut considers whether "To be? Or not to be?" Like Christ's second coming, Mr. Nut's arrival is prefigured with biblical language: "'For it is said that He will come.' Now He was coming."

40. For a general introduction to Tsiang's literary methods, see my essay, "H. T. Tsiang: Literary Innovator and Activist," in *Asian American Literature: Discourses & Pedagogies* 2 (2011), <http://onlinejournals.sjsu.edu/index.php/AALDP/article/view/84>.

Appendix

Since H. T. Tsiang self-published most of his works, including this novel, he did not have access to the design and marketing resources of a typical publishing house. This practical deprivation fostered, however, creative independence. Hence the paratexts that follow contain traces of eccentricity and genius. They are also the work of a supreme hustler who bent rules of style and propriety. The skeptical might consider these efforts merely self-promotional. The sympathetic would consider them necessary in the face of a system designed to filter out radical visions.

The following paratexts to *The Hanging on Union Square* include:

A. the first edition's cover
B. the original front matter, including
   1. excerpts from letters to Tsiang that he repurposed into blurbs
   2. excerpts from rejection letters to Tsiang from various publishers
   3. a foreword by Waldo Frank
   4. Tsiang's note of thanks to readers

and

C. a final appeal from Tsiang to his readers that appeared in the original back matter.

It is published! In its second printing!

SO

YES

the reader of a book
is more of a book
than the book is a book

I say ——

NO

SO ——

And——

The Hanging on Union Square ■ H. T. Tsiang

"I am a good deal interested in what you have tried to do, though I do not feel that the attempt has been wholly successful. As I understand it, your aim is to write a kind of Communist *Pilgrim's Progress*. This seems to me a rather surprising aim, but what you have done shows that the idea has possibilities."

GRANVILLE HICKS

"I read your book with very great interest and wish you the best of luck with it."

LOUIS ADAMIC

"The note of defiance, the revolutionary spirit in this interest me; it is an interesting experiment."

THOMAS H. UZZELL

"I have read *The Hanging on Union Square* (which, by the way, seems to me a wonderful title) and I believe that the book, although perhaps not likely to be widely read, is original and amusing."

CARL VAN DOREN

Since I didn't attend high school in this country, I read "Pilgrim's Progress" only after receiving G. H.'s letter.

H.T.

"We have not been able to convince ourselves that we could secure for the material a sufficiently extended sale to render the publication remunerative."

G. P. PUTNAM'S SONS, MINTON, BALCH & CO.

"We have decided against making you an offer of publication inasmuch as we do not believe we can sell it successfully."

LITTLE, BROWN & COMPANY

"Though we find it both entertaining and original we do not feel that its sales would justify publication."

COWARD, McCANN, *Inc.*

"It seems to us an interesting work for which there is at best only a very small public. However, we hope, for your sake, that we are mistaken in the latter point."

THE VANGUARD PRESS

"Several of us have read the manuscript carefully, and have enjoyed doing so. Unfortunately, no one of us feels sufficiently enthusiastic about this allegory to recommend that we publish it."

HARCOURT, BRACE AND COMPANY

"The idea of the book is an interesting one but we are afraid you are never going to be able to get it published as long as it remains in its present form. . . . We suggest that you re-write the story in straight-forward terms as a realistic novel."

COVICI, FRIEDE. *Publishers*

Foreword

H. T. TSIANG is a young proletarian Chinese writer of authentic value. His "Poems of the Chinese Revolution" contain verses that sing from the deep heart of the folk and that convey the passion of the world conflict. His short novel "China Red" is distinguished by its poignant, accurate lyricism and by a humor at once terrible and tender. Now Mr. Tsiang has written a satiric allegory, a *potpourri* of narrative and song, entitled "The Hanging on Union Square." As a whole, I should not say that this ambitious work is a success; and it contains passages that may offend by their crudity and by the *naïveté* of their presentation. But the book is original in form without being labored; and it is remarkable for its whimsical insights into various strata of society and for its flashing counterpoint of almost savage sensuality and delicate pity. Throughout, it is alive and evocative. And it is a harbinger of the unguessed treasures of imagination which will be released by our proletarian writers when they are freed as Mr. Tsiang is freed, of the straight-jacket of what calls itself "Marxist realism" and of what is truly a stereotype alien to both Marx and literature, and as deadening as any other dogma. Mr. Tsiang's fanciful and often fantastic visions of the workers on Union Square and of the parasites in neighboring night clubs and office buildings—while too simplistic to become high art—nevertheless convey more truth than a shelf of reportorial novels.

WALDO FRANK

I employed the method of "Socialistic Realism and Revolutionary Romanticism" when I wrote the novel.—H. T.

The writer takes this opportunity of conveying his deep appreciation of the kindness of the various critics and publishers who have read his manuscript and have given their valuable opinions of it—though these opinions may differ, more or less, here and there, now and then, from his own; and the writer is taking the liberty of asserting his own viewpoint by publishing *The Hanging on Union Square* himself i.e., stubbornly or nuttily—as he did his other two books; and the writer is willing to be judged by the text of his book, with which he has experimented, and the writer is convinced that the reaction of the masses can't be wrong.

H.T.

While getting subscriptions in preparing for the publication of *The Hanging on Union Square,* the author received many inquiries about his previous two books, *Poems of the Chinese Revolution,* published in 1929, of which only 7,000 copies have been printed, and the novel, *China Red,* published in 1931, of which only 7,100 copies have been printed; and, therefore, the author takes the present opportunity of stating that both these books are out of print now, owing to lack of funds needed for retaining type and making new plates, and that those readers who are interested in these two past works, if they send in their names and addresses, will be notified when new editions are brought out; moreover, the writer would highly appreciate any assistance given towards the circulation of the present book, so that he would be provided with the time to complete his fourth work, *Shanghai Newyork Moscow—An Odyssey of a Chinese Coolie;* for it took him only two months to write his first book but two years to distribute it; four months to write his second book, but two years also to distribute it; two months to write his third book, now in the reader's hands, but two years in preparing its publication (the process of circulating his books has been very educational although it has consumed the author's time luxuriously); furthermore, it has often been said that books, like umbrellas, when loaned, seldom come back, so let your friend spend something for something, if it is something, and automatically the writer will be benefited in paying the printer's bills sooner, and you will naturally keep your copy as you want to do—not with the intention of selling that copy for many hundreds or thousands of dollars in some time to come; but as an evidence of the realization that publishers, too, are capitalists and that proletarian literature can be produced without them, and without being straight-jacketed by them; and since the first Five Year Plan was a success, the second one can't be otherwise.

H.T.
March 1st, 1935
Box 66, Station D, N. Y. City.

Notes

ACT I

1. John D. Rockefeller (1839–1937), U.S. industrialist and philanthropist, founded Standard Oil Company. At the peak of his fortunes in 1912, Rockefeller held $900,000,000 in assets, most of which he had given away by the time he died.
2. The Young Communist League, which was established in 1921, recruited youths for ultimate participation in the Communist Party.
3. Miss Stubborn probably belonged to the Local 22 Dressmakers Union of the International Ladies Garment Workers Union (ILGWU), which was initially founded by Jewish, Italian, and Irish immigrants. Many Jews came to the United States to escape pogroms in Russia. While Miss Stubborn may or may not be Russian or Jewish, Mr. Nut believes that she has associated herself with them via her politics. The successful strike mentioned in the novel may have occurred in New York on August 16, 1933.
4. Grover Whalen (1886–1962) served as New York City's Police Commissioner from 1928 until 1930. He established a police academy and used undercover agents to break up communist groups in the city. Whalen also prospered as the general manager of Wanamaker's Department Store.
5. These men make an unlikely trio, since Norman Thomas (1884–1968)—called "Mister" on p. 42—was a socialist and pacifist; J. P. Morgan, Jr. (1867–1943) was a financier, like his father; and John J. Pershing (1860–1948) was military commander of U.S. forces in Europe during World War I. Thomas did, however, meet with Morgan's partner, Thomas W. Lamont, in 1931 to discuss how the business community could address the plight of the poor (W. A. Swanberg, *Norman Thomas: The Last Idealist* [New York: Scribners, 1976], p. 124). John J. Pershing's tenuous connection to Thomas involves his minor role in sponsoring a

controversial event in 1934 featuring the latter as the speaker ("U.S. Chamber Bars Town Hall Forum," *New York Times*, December 5, 1934, p. 25). Tsiang may have perceived all three as public figures standing in the way of his political goals: Thomas's socialism opposed Tsiang's more radical aims; Morgan both opposed communism and financed the Japanese government; and Pershing led a military whose actions Tsiang seldom approved.

6. These terms—"strenuous competition" and "adapting herself to her environment"—are drawn from the theory of social Darwinism, popular in America during the late nineteenth and early twentieth centuries, which held that the laws of natural selection developed by Charles Darwin to describe the evolution of species applied also to individuals and social groups.

7. The *New Pioneer* was the official organ of the Young Pioneers of America, a group for communists aged 8 to 15 (Elizabeth Kirpatrick Dilling, *The Red Network* [1934. New York: Arno, 1977], pp. 249–250).

8. A reference to the Soviet practice, first introduced in 1928, of planning change in five-year increments.

9. Franklin Delano Roosevelt (1882–1945) served as president of the United States of America from 1933 until 1945. Norman Thomas (1884–1968) was a prominent socialist and founder of the organization that would become the American Civil Liberties Union; Leon Trotsky (1879–1940), a leader of the Bolshevik Revolution, was exiled from the Soviet Union in 1929 by Joseph Stalin, who headed that country from 1924 until 1953. Jay Lovestone (1897–1990) briefly led the Communist Party of the USA but was ousted in 1929 and ultimately led anti-communist organizations.

10. For $2, Tsiang peddled copies of his first novel, *China Red* (1931), at various cafeterias and other gathering places in New York City.

11. The Trade Union Unity League founded the National Unemployed Council in 1930.

12. A quotation that may be attributable to Linus Price Hayes (1906–1966), editor of the *Skipper*, a magazine published at Virginia Polytechnic Institute from 1927 until 1934.

13. A cheapskate.

14. In the 1930s, the leftist International Labor Defense worked to overturn the convictions of nine black men who had been accused of raping two white women in Scottsboro, Alabama. Irving Plaza, located at Irving Place and Fifteenth Street in New

York City, served as a meeting place for leftists and as a performance space for Tsiang's plays.

15. An era during which the high valuation of mechanical devices is perceived by some to be directly proportional to the devaluation of people, though Miss Digger uses the term more generically to mean a modern era.

16. A socialist periodical published in New York since 1924 by the American Labor Conference on International Affairs.

17. A reference either to the company that Morgan founded or to Morgan Jr., since John Pierpont Morgan himself—an investment banker with holdings in several industries including railroads, electric companies, and steel manufacturers—died in 1913.

18. Slang for policemen.

ACT II

1. Located on 507 West Street in New York City, this establishment, sponsored by the American Seamen's Friends Society, offered food and shelter to destitute sailors.

2. The section of Lower Manhattan in New York City that served as the center of the city's theater life in the 1860s and 1870s. By the 1880s, it had become an economically depressed area.

3. A system in which block chairmen would solicit donations of 10 cents to $1 a week for twenty weeks from residents of a block to assist unemployed people and their families in New York. By April 1932, 7597 blocks were officially organized in the Bronx, Manhattan, Brooklyn, and Queens ("Block Aid Covers Whole City," *New York Times*, April 1, 1932).

4. Sometimes poets would post or read aloud their poetry in a public place such as Union Square or Washington Square, where Tsiang himself posted his work in 1933 ("'Village' Pegasus Gallops for Coins of Bourgeoisie," *Washington Post*, May 22, 1933).

5. Tammany Hall is another name for the executive committee of the Democratic Party in New York City, which secured its considerable power in the nineteenth and early twentieth centuries through bribery and other kinds of corruption.

6. Max Eastman (1883–1969), U.S. writer and editor of such radical periodicals as *The Masses* and *The Liberator*.

7. The professor's exclamations reference the titles of two books written by Oswald Spengler and translated from the German by Charles Francis Atkinson: *The Decline of the West* (1926–1928)

and *The Hour of Decision: Germany and World-Historical Evolution* (1934).

8. Al Capone (1899–1947), a leader of organized crime in Chicago, was arrested in 1931 for federal income-tax evasion, eventually serving time at the Atlanta Federal Penitentiary as prisoner number 40886 before being transferred to Alcatraz ("Al Capone Loses Identity in Prison," *New York Times*, May 6, 1932).

9. Members of Hitler's Nazi Party came to be known as Brown Shirts for the color of their uniform. Mr. Ratsky imagines that his followers would wear a lighter hue.

10. J. P. Morgan and J. D. Rockefeller.

11. In 1932, the total number of unemployed persons in America was 12,060,000 according to "Employment Status of the Civilian Population, 1929–2002," *Statistical Abstract of the United States* (2003), p. 50.

12. According to *Cassel's Dictionary of Slang*, "pizzicato" in the 1930s served as an adjective meaning "tipsy." Miss Digger appears to be using it as a noun here, perhaps as a term of endearment like "silly."

13. New York City averages 0.5 inches of snow in April.

14. John D. Rockefeller.

15. The Congressional Medal of Honor is the highest award for valor that the United States can bestow upon a member of its armed forces. On May 23, 1932, Amelia Earhart (1897–1937) was recommended for a Congressional Medal for being the first woman to fly solo across the Atlantic Ocean.

16. The communist organ, *The Daily Worker*, had its offices at 50 East Thirteenth Street.

17. Communists and labor unions sometimes met and organized at Webster Hall on 119 East Eleventh Street.

18. Implying that the prosperity some Americans enjoyed during the 1920s would continue and even expand, the Republican National Committee used this slogan to promote the presidential candidacy of Herbert Hoover in 1928, though Hoover himself never used it in his own campaign speeches.

19. Prohibition ended in 1933.

20. A song written by W. C. Handy in 1914 featuring blues, ragtime, church music, and habanera rhythms. Directed by Dudley Murphy, singer Bessie Smith starred in a short-film version of the song, which ran before feature films from 1929 until 1932. See Will Friedwald, *Stardust Melodies: The Biography of Twelve of*

America's Most Popular Songs (New York: Pantheon, 2002), pp. 39–74.

ACT III

1. These slogans were used by Burma-Shave in the 1930s.
2. On March 7, 1932, four demonstrators were killed and more than sixty were injured at a strike at the Ford Motor Company's plant in Detroit, Michigan.
3. The Acme Theater on the corner of Broadway and Fourth Avenue showed Soviet films from 1921 until it was demolished in 1934.
4. An equestrian statue of George Washington (1732–1799) by Henry Kirke Brown.
5. Mr. Nut imagines Frédéric-Auguste Bartholdi's bronze statue of the Marquis de Lafayette (1757–1834) speaking French to him: "Would you like to buy, good sir, my beautiful young woman? Thank you very much, good Nut. Good evening. Good morning."
6. Mr. Nut imagines the statue of Abraham Lincoln (1809–1865)—also by Henry Kirke Brown—giving his famous Gettysburg Address (1863).
7. The U.S. Navy used this touristic recruiting slogan, but the Army did not promise "a ball game." In the 1930s, the Army, like the Navy, advertised travel opportunities, as well as a steady paycheck. See John B. Mitchell, "Army Recruiters and Recruits between the World Wars," *Military Collector and Historian* 19.3 (1967), pp. 76–81.
8. According to the *New York Times*, the Polish American artist Gan Kolski leapt to his death on April 18, 1932.
9. According to the *New York Times*, the unidentified man leapt from this height on November 13, 1932.
10. Reno, Nevada, was a favorite spot for eager couples who took advantage of the state's no-waiting period for issuing marriage licenses.
11. A United Front formed in the 1930s when communists allied with other radical groups against common enemies such as fascism.
12. A member of the Soviet state police.
13. Unlike Britain and other countries that abandoned the gold standard in 1931 in favor of imposing foreign exchange controls, France attempted to defend the value of the gold franc until 1936.

Hence, France's share of the world's gold reserves rose from 7% in 1926 to 27% in 1932.

14. Benito Mussolini (1883–1945), fascist Italian prime minister from 1922–1943.

15. Northeastern region of China, parts of which the Japanese government controlled from 1905 until 1931, and all of which was under Japanese colonial rule from 1932 until 1945.

16. Articulated by U.S. Secretary of State John Hay in 1899, the Open Door Policy stipulated that Chinese ports should be open equally to all nations trading with China.

17. Vladimir Ilich Lenin (1870–1924) headed the Bolshevik wing of the Russian Social-Democratic Workers' Party and led the Bolshevik Revolution in 1917.

18. A federally funded welfare program administered during the Depression.

ACT IV

1. On February 15, 1933, Giuseppe Zangara (1900–1933) attempted to assassinate President-elect Franklin D. Roosevelt in Miami, Florida.

2. A confusing statement. Perhaps Nut is referring to the fifty-nine U.S. senators of the Democratic Party, FDR's party, in 1933.

3. The official newspaper of the American Communist Party, published between 1924 and 1957.

4. Dedicated in 1930, this flagpost was meant to honor Tammany president Charles F. Murphy. Public sentiment was against this name, however, so it became known as Independence Flagstaff, one of the largest in New York State at the time.

5. The commonly known name of the prison in Ossining, New York.

6. The popular name for FDR's group of political advisors.

7. Reference to Pearl S. Buck (1892–1973), the daughter of American missionaries in China, who wrote *The Good Earth* (1931), a novel about a Chinese farming family.

8. Pearl S. Buck's novel *Sons* (1932) features a character named Wang the Tiger, a warlord who conquers one section of a northern province in China.

9. According to the U.S. War Department, 8,528,831 soldiers on both sides of World War I were killed, while 21,189,154 were wounded. Estimates hold that more than 13,000,000 civilians died as a result of the war.

10. The practice of compelling employees to work faster in order to increase profit.
11. Located on 490 Riverside Drive, the church features a 392-foot tall gothic-style steeple.
12. This line is taken from the 1929 song "Happy Days Are Here Again" by Milton Ager and Jack Yellen. It served as the song for FDR's successful presidential campaign in 1932.
13. The Jewish moneylender in Shakespeare's play *The Merchant of Venice* (1600).

America Is in the Heart

Carlos Bulosan's semi-autobiographical classic remains one of the most influential texts on the Filipino American experience and the plight of migrant laborers in the United States pre–World War II. Vividly recalling the intense racial abuse in the fields, towns, cities, and canneries of California and the Pacific Northwest during the 1930s, *America Is in the Heart* shows what it was like to be criminalized as a migrant yet drawn to the ideals America symbolized.

"Bulosan's novel is indispensable—so is confronting what lies in it." –Elaine Castillo, from the Foreword

East Goes West

Having left Korea for the gleaming promise of the United States, the young Chungpa Han lands in New York with little to his name. Struggling to support his studies, he becomes by turns a traveling salesman, a domestic worker, and a farmer, and observes firsthand the idealism and greed of the industrializing twentieth century. Part picaresque adventure, part social commentary, *East Goes West* casts a sharply satirical eye on the demands and perils of assimilation.

"Groundbreaking and inspirational . . . A call to action, a call for the country to live up to the dream it has of itself . . . This book is for all of us." –Alexander Chee, from the Foreword

Printed in the United States
by Baker & Taylor Publisher Services